Confer

By Hamish

CW00508136

Conference by Hamish McBain Published Internationally by Marvin Press – PO Box 14, Cundletown, NSW, 2430, Australia.

This book is a work of fiction. Any similarity between the characters and situations within it's pages and places or persons, living or dead, is unintentional and co-incidental.

Chapter 1

Cameron Woods woke from a sweaty, cramped sleep. He was knackered and his body felt like it had been hit by a bus. He'd been sitting in the same position for the last fourteen hours as Flight 202 had flown around the world from Singapore to Scotland. This was the second leg of the long trek from Sydney, Australia to Edinburgh. He was supposed to spend three hours in Singapore but due to "Adverse Weather Conditions" had spent seven hours staring at orchids and other pissed off travellers waiting to board the delayed flight.

He slowly became aware of the activity around him. Stewards were collecting uneaten meals. Passengers were queueing in aisles for toilets carrying toilet bags and tooth brushes. Other passengers tried for those last few precious minutes of sleep wearing black sleep masks and hiding under blankets. He realised he badly needed to pee but the size of the queues made him believe that he could hold on until Edinburgh...assuming they were there soon.

The intercom crackled and a voice speaking in Singaporean English announced that due to congestion at Edinburgh Airport the plane was now about to commence a holding pattern circling to the north of the city and would land when Air Traffic Control permitted...time till landing approximately forty-five minutes.

Cameron rose and stretched and joined the queue to the nearest toilet hoping he wouldn't pee until it was his turn. Once his mission was accomplished he climbed back into his seat. As the plane circled over the Kingdom of Fife and the Firth of Forth, Cameron contemplated his previous adventures in Scotland's capital city.

He had studied Veterinary Medicine and Surgery at Glasgow University about an hour west along the M8 motorway. The rivalry between the two Vet Schools – Glasgow and Edinburgh – was legendary. Annual sports days were days of epic rugby matches and monstrous drinking sessions. He had been part of the victorious First Fifteen who had beaten Edinburgh - in Edinburgh – for the first time in almost 30 years. 1984 – A glorious year… the year before he qualified as a vet. He had had no idea how to play rugby but, back in the day, he had been a great sprinter. Captain William P O'Shaunessy had told him if he got the ball just to run like buggery… And run like buggery he did. He didn't score but made precious yards again and again before be being carried off the park concussed late in the second half. There were no team doctors or hospital visits back in those days and Cameron was nursed back to health with rigorous fluid therapy… somewhere in the region of fifteen or sixteen pints Tennent's Lager over the next few hours… This was a legendary day…night…weekend… but even now, decades later, Cameron only new the legend through the accounts of others. His memories after the match only start when he woke up in his sick bed in Glasgow two days later.

Every visit to Edinburgh involved alcohol. The pubs were wonderful. Rose street was wonderful – 24 pubs in one mile – all vibrant and electric. Edinburgh University was wonderful – ancient and beautiful with student bars filled with music and laughter. There was beer everywhere. The amber fluid delicious and refreshing and often the starting point for great adventures.

In recent years he had returned with his family and friends for Buck's Nights, weddings and christenings…always celebrations…always beer. Beautiful Edinburgh was simply the greatest watering hole on the planet.

The boys in the 1984 First Fifteen were still some of his best friends. They had all met during "Freshers Week" at Glasgow University in 1980, a week where all new students arrived from across the UK and beyond to meet each other and bond before the serious chore of studying started. It was a week of fun and alcoholic madness.

He had met Randal Hollingsworth and Peter McEwan on the very first day during a tour of Garscube Estate – the large beautiful green estate in Bearsden, a rather posh outer suburb of Glasgow where Glasgow Veterinary School is situated.

Randal a tall, well built, curly headed English git with a stupid accent had come from a private boarding school in the midlands of England. He hadn't obtained high enough grades in his school exams to get into the English Veterinary Schools – London, Cambridge, Bristol or Liverpool – but Glasgow had welcomed him with open arms... much to his parent's dismay. He was a powerful man in a scrum and played Lock.

Peter was a very different kettle of fish. He was lean and wiry with short cropped dark hair and steel blue eyes. He was a very loud catholic Glaswegian. He loved Celtic Football Club and could drink like a fish. He was only 17 years old and could still drink like a fish. Thank goodness for acne pock marks making him look seriously older than he was... and fake ID which could be readily obtained from some of Peter's dodgy contacts at St. Aloysius Academy in central Glasgow. Peter was from a solid working class background and was an extremely nice guy... Just loud... Way too loud. As a scrum half he was fantastic.

Cameron, Peter and Randal hit it off like a house on fire and on that very first night ended up blind drunk in the "Beer Bar" in the Men's Union at the main University campus in town. Peter had led the singing from on top of the beer sodden table – introducing his new mates to beautiful songs such as "Father Abraham" and "My rhubarb refuses to rise..." both of which involved the entire population of the bar climbing onto the tables and screaming choruses while smashing tin beer trays against the ceiling. A great night and no arrests. The Men's Union had actually seen it all before.

In the days to come others joined the trio. Logan Bloomsberry – another posh, big English git with a blonde mop of hair, blue twinkling eyes, stupid accent and a fat arse found the threesome hilarious and the merry band grew. Logan's height and big arse made him a good choice as the other Lock in the scrum.

William P O'Shaunessy an Irish Private School boy from Ballymena, built like a brick shit house with a face already rearranged by too many rugby injuries, fitted very snugly into the group. From the outset everyone loved him. He was soft hearted and funny and a true gentleman. William could have played rugby professionally as a full back. He was a born leader. He was captain courageous for the Vet School First Fifteen and he drove his team to undreamed heights, leading by example, playing ferociously and fairly. With William as full back the team was invincible.

Mick O'Reilly and Gregor Alcott – two protestant Northern Irish kids became immersed in the group towards the end of the week. Mick short and stumpy and Gregor six foot three and lean were both sharp with caustic wit. Their religious banter with Peter and William who were both devout Catholics sometimes seemed to stretch the new friendship but by Saturday night when they all stood on the beer bar tables and sang "The Sash" – a protestant Orangemen anthem, they were going to be solid friends for ever. Mick was a formidable hooker and Gregor was a greyhound like winger with great fast hands.

Quietly both Harold Ainsley and Damien Corrigan slid into the group. Harold was from an extremely posh English private school in Oxford. He had shining, coiffured blond hair and cherubic red lips. He didn't seem to fit very well with the bunch – maybe they weren't good enough for him -but he hung around on the periphery and slowly became a regular. He never played rugby but was always present at matches and the after parties. It seemed like he just thought he should be there.

Damien Corrigan was a small hairy guy from Liverpool. Nothing posh about Damien – he was from a rough public school but had scored higher grades in his final exams than anyone else in the school's history. He was quiet and shy but quietly loved the humour of the outgoing boys in the bunch. He came to be treated like a little brother by everyone in the group. He was another true gentleman. Dave played fly half and had a great rugby brain - second only to William.

There were a few girls floating around during that first week but the boys were too busy bonding and trying to impress each other to notice. The hangovers were ridiculous. The money pissed down the urinal was huge... but in the end well worth it. Lifelong friendships were being forged. They were having the time of their lives.

Chapter 2

The plane's public address system crackled into life once more. "We regret that due to congestion at Edinburgh Airport we have still not received authorisation to land and will continue our holding pattern until further notice from air traffic control... For those of you travelling on connecting flights from Edinburgh please contact our cabin crew..."

There was an audible groan from the frustrated passengers on board. Everyone looked bored, tired and frustrated. Several passengers were berating the cabin staff who looked as frustrated as they did. Kids were crying. Overhead lockers were being opened and closed and baggage rearranged. People were cursing in toilet queues. No one was amused. Flight 202 from Singapore was no longer a reflection of Singapore Airlines TV commercials with happy, relaxed, beaming passengers and gorgeous air hostesses smiling happily without a hair out of place.

Cameron groaned and closed his eyes. This was a great way to start his Scottish trip. His plan was to spend the first 5 days in Edinburgh at the World Small Animal Veterinary Association conference – WSAVA annual conference - at the Edinburgh International Conference Centre, and then hire a car and travel up the coast to Aberdeen to spend a couple of weeks with his parents and brothers. He was supposed to have arrived early Sunday morning, which would have given him a quiet day at his hotel in Edinburgh to sleep and refresh, before heading to the conference centre for opening night drinks and registration. At this rate he might miss the opening night events all together. He had no idea what time of day it was in Edinburgh but it had to be getting late in the day.... He was booked into the Sheraton Grand Hotel on Festival square. The web info had stated it was only 200 metres walk from the conference centre and was offering good rates to WSAVA members. It did look very nice. He hoped that there would be conference delegates he knew staying at the hotel too. Hopefully some of his old crew from Uni days.

An air hostess brushed passed his arm and continued up the aisle towards the forward galley. He opened his eyes and watched the nice curve of her small buttocks, tightly covered in Singapore Airlines fabric, wiggle away from him. Very nice he thought... Very nice... But the thought only deepened his developing bad mood. He stared at the tantalising bottom and then closed his eyes again.

He was travelling on his own. His wife of 25 years, Alison, had not wanted to come on this trip. She usually loved veterinary adventures – especially overseas. She loved exploring host cities and being a tourist. She loved the social events. She was always delighted to meet up with other vet's wives. She loved evening drinks with the delegates. She loved dressing up for formal dinners and was often the life and soul of conference functions. She usually had a ball. Happy, effervescent Alison.

At 48 years old she was a very attractive woman. She was very slim with beautiful long wavy blonde hair. She still had beautiful pale unblemished skin with a lovely smattering of tan freckles highlighting her high cheek bones, small button nose, large blue eyes and sculpted lips. Her smile was dazzling with perfect teeth that were whiter than white. She was gorgeous. Her biggest complaint about herself year after year was that God hadn't given her a bust. Her bottom was OK – not too small and not too big... But she really longed for bigger boobs. Cameron didn't care. He loved boobs of any size or shape.

Alison had declined the offer of the overseas trip. "Too much going on at home." The local tennis finals were coming up and she was through to the quarter finals in both the singles and the mixed doubles. If she came she would miss an endurance ride in Katoomba in the Blue Mountains and "Johnny", her 12 year old quarter horse gelding, was in the best form of his life. Besides that she couldn't miss Stephanie Cassegrain's 50th birthday bash – her husband had hired a house in the Hunter Valley for the weekend and they were going to have an absolute ball.

Alison didn't work any more. When Cameron first met her she worked as a Physiotherapist in Aiden Falls – a small tourist town about fifteen kilometres from Katoomba. Cameron had set up his Veterinary Practice there two years beforehand. That was twenty-seven years ago.

He had been kicked by a cow and had broken two metatarsal bones in his right hand. He needed physiotherapy to get back to work fast. Alison, who was locuming at the physiotherapy practice in Aiden Falls at the time, fell head over heels in love with her patient. This good looking young Vet with the unintelligible Scottish accent was her dream man. She moved in with Cameron after three months of dating and they were married a year later.

She continued to work part-time for 3-4 years after the wedding. When they realised that they were having problems falling pregnant Alison gave up work to relax and spend time concentrating on reproduction. They tried continually for several years to have a baby naturally and then completed several rounds of IVF with no joy. Eventually they resigned themselves to the realisation that they weren't meant to have kids. Maybe it would happen when they weren't trying so hard... It never did. Alison never went back to work. Cameron's practice grew substantially – the large animal component reduced over time due to the growth of the town and the reduction in farm land as tourism took hold of the Blue Mountains. The up side was that the small animal component of the practice grew dramatically. By 2000 he had employed 2 more vets and financially Aiden Falls Veterinary Hospital was doing rather well. Alison did not have to work to contribute to the Woods' family budget and now realised that she rather enjoyed not working.

For the last 16 years Alison had kept house and cooked every meal for Cameron. She looked after him extremely well. She filled her days playing tennis, kayaking, horse-riding and attending social functions all over the Blue Mountains. Her circle of friends included all the "right people" – wives of doctors and lawyers and business women in the local area. She seemed to cultivate her social set carefully. Cameron didn't mind – he was friends with them all anyway. She was always extremely busy and never had a moment to relax.

In the last 18 months their relationship had undergone a subtle change. She was still the vibrant bubbly Alison of old but her amorous encounters with Cameron had slowly diminished. Alison was not as interested in sex as she had been in years gone by. Once Cameron had wondered if she had cystic ovaries as she behaved like a nymphomaniac demanding sex not only everyday but sometimes 2 or three times a day.

Nothing to complain about there apart from a chaffed penis on occasion. In the old days he treated cows for nymphomania with hormones. These cows usually had large cysts on their ovaries producing oestrogens which kept them on heat for weeks even months if untreated. These cows would stand to be ridden by bulls and even other females day after day after day... Hormone treatment and manual rupture of the offending cysts would often have the cow back to normal three weekly cycling within a few days. He suspected the medics who dealt with his and Alison's infertility problems would have checked this out fairly early in their investigations and treated it accordingly if it was indeed a factor. After 2-3 years of constant daily bonking life settled into what Cameron thought was relatively normal... 2-3 bonks a week with extra good times on birthdays and Xmas. In the last 18 month however things had slowed dramatically.

Cameron was lucky if he got a nookie a month in the last year and a half. Alison seemed totally disinterested. She seemed to go through the motions. There was no enthusiasm. She never initiated the act. The last bonk he had before flying to Scotland had been at least 6 weeks ago and he thought it was like shagging a bag of spuds. He wondered if she had died underneath him there was so little movement as he reached for an explosive crescendo... Then a small voice asked, "Are you finished yet?" He was totally deflated.

"Em... no dear..."

"Can you hurry up and get on with it? I'm really tired..."

Cameron had wiggled for a few more confused seconds and then slid back to his side of the bed without the earth moving in any way at all. Alison had rolled over and was snoring within a couple of minutes.

Cameron had been devastated and extremely confused. He didn't sleep that night. When he had broached the subject of her lack of libido in the months before she had blamed menopause and "changes that women go through..." She was 48 years old – he didn't know if this was menopause or not. She confused him to buggery. When out socialising she was still the life of every party – she was loud, sexy and naughty. She flirted with every male in their social circle – some more than others... But she'd always done this. Was she putting on an act for everyone or was she now bored with just him... Was she rooting somebody else? Fuck. Maybe he wasn't man enough for her. He hadn't provided her with kids... But shit he'd provided her with everything else... A beautiful house, a fantastic lifestyle, a bloody big horse, overseas holidays... He'd given her a free reign to do whatever she wanted... Fuck... Was he missing something? He had worshipped her for years. He still worshipped her. He loved her insanely. She was the only woman he had ever loved.

Whatever was going on he felt lonely and betrayed. What on earth was he missing? Was she screwing somebody else behind his back? Did everybody else know besides him?

She was still beautiful. She was still bright and bubbly... until they were on their own together. Surely menopause would affect her all the time – her public face as well as her private face... Or was she just making a huge effort for everyone else. Fuck.

He had looked back on the previous 12-18 months of his life and realised he had been lonely in his own home for a very long time.

Chapter 3

There was a general commotion in the airplane. People were stowing bags in overhead lockers and clicking and fastening seatbelts. Cameron had dosed off and was only vaguely aware of the announcement over the PA system. He assumed that a landing announcement had been made. The lovely face of a very pretty Singaporean air hostess leaned into his vision and checked that his seatbelt was fastened. As she turned to check the passengers in front he gazed at another lovely bottom outlined in air hostess uniform. This one was markedly larger than the first which had caught his eye earlier. Nevertheless it was still a lovely shape. He contemplated how he liked arses of all shapes and sizes. As long as it belonged to a female. Any arse in a storm he thought. Was he mixing his metaphors?

As the descent started he contemplated a thought which had been trying very hard to break into his conscious for quite some time. He realised that he really wanted a shag. He was on his own, half a world away from his normal life and he really wanted a shag. Was it a desire for pure excitement – just to misbehave? Was he just desperate for sex? Did he want some sort of revenge for how he had been treated lately? Did he want anonymous sex with someone unknown that he would never meet again...? Or was it actually sex he was after? Did he just want to hold and caress somebody? Did he simply want to feel the warmth of another human being? Did he want to feel close to someone – feel a connection? He didn't know what he wanted. He felt a combination of excitement and guilt even contemplating these thoughts.

There were women he was hoping to meet at this conference but had no idea if they would be there. They were all his class mates from uni days. He genuinely wanted to see them and find out how they were going in life. He wanted to see that they were well and that their kids were well and growing up happily. For each of them he had a quiet longing that they would be lonely like him and want to drag him off to bed and ravage him for days on end. He pretended to himself that this was not the case but he knew, that given half a chance, he wasn't going to refuse an invitation or avoid an opportunity.

He wondered if Jacqueline Alcott would be across from Northern Ireland. She had been Cameron's girlfriend throughout the five years at Glasgow University. Back in the day, fresh from secondary school in Halifax she was so gorgeous. She had long curly brown hair and toffee coloured brown eyes, nice lips and squint teeth – back before every kid was fitted with braces by the time they were 10. She was voluptuous. She had an hour glass figure and absolutely scrumptious boobs and a perfect arse. She was hyper intelligent and very, very sexy. She was also a psychotic bitch. Cameron had fallen for her feminine charms early in first year and had been totally smitten. She was extremely manipulative. In second year, when the relationship was going south and Cameron decided that they should part, she'd threatened suicide. Cameron stayed. For the next 4 years she threatened suicide every time they had a hiccup. Cameron stayed with Jacqueline because of her emotional blackmail throughout all their university days. In their final year, two weeks before their final exams, Cameron called in unexpectedly to Jacqueline's flat and found her shagging a dead shit medical student on the kitchen floor. Cameron told her to fuck off out of his life and she threatened suicide again. He said "Go ahead". She didn't. Cameron felt that he had just wasted four and a half years of his life.

In the coming months he discovered that Jacqui had shagged numerous other students during their bizarre relationship. Legend had it that a couple of vet school lecturers had dipped their wicks there also.

Twelve months after leaving university Cameron received a phone call from Gregor Alcott. Gregor was in the Vet school rugby team and had shared a flat with Cameron during fourth year on The Great Western Road. They were friends but had never been very close. Gregor announced that, somehow or other, Jacqueline and he had managed to get shacked up with each other and they were going to get married in 12months. He was hoping Cameron would give them his blessing. Cameron came off the phone doing back-flips... Jacqueline had continued to stalk him after university. He was elated. Now someone else had to cope with her mental health issues. Free at last.

Jacqui and Gregor married and moved to Northern Ireland. They had 2 kids – a boy and a girl. The kids would probably both be in their 20s by now. Gregor had given private practice away finding it too stressful being on call. He had worked for the government for the last 20 years or so in Animal Health...pushing pens constructing import and export protocols for the Northern Ireland government and the European Union. Jacqui worked part time in small animal practice somewhere in County Down. Facebook reliably informed Cameron that Jacqui was still very attractive. He couldn't believe she was still with Gregor. She always needed excitement back in the day. She had to be bored. Gregor had to be one of the straightest and most serious people on the planet.

With these thoughts in mind – an attractive woman plodding along in a boring marriage and the fact that she had slack morals back in the day – Cameron thought that if she attended the conference on her own – she might be keen to rekindle an old flame. Who cared if she was nuts. At least he knew the score.

Deirdre Micallef was another class mate that he would love to catch up with. She was just the most naive and gorgeous girl in the class of '85. She was petite with short black hair and dark hazel eyes. She was quite stocky and muscular but simply the nicest girl that God had put on earth. She was lovely to everyone and in return most folk were lovely to her. Cameron had fancied her all the way through Vet School but he was attached to Jacqui. Most other blokes in the year had fancied her all the way through Vet School too. Damien Corrigan had worshipped her. He tried so hard to win her heart but just kept pushing the wrong buttons. It was a great shame – they could have been perfect together. Damien the world's hairiest gentleman and everyone's little brother - and Deirdre – the prettiest and sweetest kid on the block... But the chemistry was wrong. Deirdre had had a couple of bad relationships with older students during her years in Glasgow and had left after graduation to work on the Shetland Isles. There she had met a lovely sheep farmer and they had married and had three delightful kids. Tragically her husband had been diagnosed with Parkinson's disease almost 15 years ago. Deirdre was a selfless carer and now only worked part-time at the practice she had worked at since 1985.

Cameron wanted to see her out of genuine affection for her. He hoped her life was as good as it could be. He also wanted to talk to her about poor Damien Corrigan. Although she never dated him, he was sure that they would have kept in contact. Damien had tragically committed suicide almost 2 years ago now. Cameron had problems getting his head around his little friend's death and he thought Deirdre might be a good person to chew the fat with.

In the back of his mind he wondered what her love life was like these days. Was she now in a marriage that was cruel to her? Did she yearn for some physical release? If she needed some quiet comforting he would be happy to oblige. If she needed some wild exuberant comforting he would also be happy to oblige. These thoughts actually pained him. He felt guilty for thinking them. But...

Cameron hoped above all that Shona Hollingsworth would be at the conference. Back then she had been Shona Soutar. At University Shona had been everybody's sister. She was short and blonde with beautiful Scottish pale skin and twinkling light blue eyes. She had a tiny bum but the greatest set of boobs in the history of the universe. Shakespeare had written sonnets about them. Ulysses would have travelled another Odyssey for them. Neil Armstrong went to the moon just to get a better view of them. They were legendary. They were sculpted onto her torso in such a way that they simply defied gravity - beautiful, round and full, and they did not droop at all. They stood out at right angles to her torso - even when she lay down. Fantastic. More importantly, Cameron and Shona had been great friends back in the Glasgow days. He was attached to Jacqui and she was attached to Randal. That made it safe to be pals and discuss all manner of boy/girl stuff. They had discussed the universe, re written the Old Testament and the Koran and had pushed for same sex marriage 30 years ago... They had been drunk together on various occasions and taken each other home and tucked each other in bed and stayed until the others partner had arrived to take over. They had been best pals.

Shona had been swept off her feet by Randal Hollingsworth in the very first month of the first term at Uni. He was besotted by her. He had first laid eyes on her in a corridor of the Vet School between lectures and had vowed within seconds that he would make her his own. Shona was initially overwhelmed and stayed evasive but the well-built English git never gave in and within a few weeks they were an item. They were the only couple in the entire class to stay together and marry beyond Uni. They became engaged in final year. Cameron was sure that Randal was putting his stamp on Shona before she headed out into the big world beyond Garscube Estate. The year after graduating Shona got a small animal job In Wiltshire in England and Randal stayed behind at Glasgow University to do an Orthopaedic Internship.

During the next couple of years Cameron lost touch with Shona. He also worked in England but up in the Yorkshire Dales where he was extremely busy in mixed practice and working every hour that God sent. After 2 years in mixed practice in Thirsk, Cameron departed the UK and went to locum in Australia. Contact then became very irregular. Eventually Cameron received word that Shona and Randal were getting married. The timing was good. Cameron was heading home to see his family. He would be home for a month and the wedding was the third Saturday he would be home. Great timing. Randal asked if he would come down to Dunblane for the week before the wedding to give him some moral support and help with the wedding preparations. The idea was great. He was to stay with Shona's Mum and Dad's at their place. Her parents were a delight and he'd spent many weekends with them during university. He was excited and looked forward to it immensely. Once he arrived in Dunblane he realised that he was there for a reason. He was to be a human shield. He was there to deflect the flack away from Randal. In the preceding couple of months Shona had found out that Randal had been shagging students at the University where he was working. Amongst others, he had been shagging an English PhD student called Belinda. Randal was her mentor and he had been mentoring her in much more than orthopaedics. It seems they both had quite an interest in reproduction. Belinda had been invited to Shona's parents on several occasions as a friend and they had looked after her like one of their own. When Shona put two and two together all hell broke loose. Randal was shunned by the whole Soutar family. Randal though, had a silver tongue and talked Shona into going ahead with the nuptials. "It's all been a misunderstanding… There was nothing in it… It was all in Belinda's head…" Why Shona listened, Cameron had no idea. Here he was playing diplomat in a minefield. Randal had invited him here for fun and banter. He was actually here to stop Randal being strung up by the bollocks. It was a bizarre week. Over beers with Randal he realised that he was just a lying English prick. Over beers with Shona's father he had no idea what to say at all. He spent the week running for milk and groceries and inviting people to play golf or visit grandma and grandpa. When he listened to Shona explaining away how poor Randal had been a victim of circumstance he felt like running away.

The wedding was bizarre. Cameron realised that being in the southern hemisphere he had been the last to find out about Randal's indiscretions. When the rest of the troops arrived for the weekend - the rugby boys and the uni friends with new partners, boyfriends, girlfriends and spouses - they all seemed very surprised that the nuptials were actually going ahead. Cameron almost cried during the church service… not tears of joy. When Shona's father stood up at the wedding breakfast to welcome Randal to the family, Cameron had to go outside and skull Glen Fiddich till he fell over and puked. His drunken state certainly took the attention away from the bride and groom. That was what he was there for wasn't it?

Shona and Randal had eventually parted company after twenty-six years of marriage, just six months before the WSAVA conference in Edinburgh. They'd had three kids. Shona had given up work to bring up the kids and Randal had set up a huge small animal referral practice in northern Manchester. It was a gold mine – he was an orthopaedic god…but this was not enough for Randal. Five years previous to the break-up Randal had sold his share in the practice and gone into partnership with Harry Ainsley. He bought a slice of Harry's growing corporate veterinary business -"Noah's Ark Veterinary Hospitals" or "NAVHs". The business now owned and managed over 120 small animal practices throughout the whole of the UK. The marriage break up had been vitriolic. Shona was left with the house and no money in the bank and no income – she hadn't worked for over 20 years. She had sacrificed her working life to look after the kids. Randal did not care. The word on the street was that he had been shagging around for years and that he was presently shacked up with another Belinda whose title was "NAVHs Financial Manager".

There was no word than Shona had another man in her life. The kids were all at Uni. Seemingly her close friends were telling her to go back to being a vet. Hopefully she'd turn up at the conference. Probably not. Maybe someone could fill him in on what she was up to.

God! If she turned up he'd love to see her. Love to mull over the last 20 odd years with her. He'd always thought she was beautiful. He wondered if her boobs still defied gravity. It might be a while since she's had a bonk. She might be as horny as a toad... His mind wandered back to a cheapo holiday all the troops had taken after graduation on the Costa-Del-Sol. They were on the beach. Shona appeared in a white almost see-through bikini. He had to lie face down on his towel for about half an hour after talking to her at close quarters. His stiffy had almost torn a hole in his speedos.

His reverie was rudely interrupted as the wheels of the aircraft bumped onto the tarmac at Edinburgh Airport. The cabin of the large aircraft was gently bounced up and down for a few seconds until the gentle roar of the engines, powering onto reverse thrust, announced the slowing of the large vehicle to a relaxed crawl.

"Local time here is 1440 – please adjust your watches and phones." Only 8 hours late.

"Thank you for Flying with Singapore Airlines. Welcome to Edinburgh – the capital of Scotland"

Chapter 4

As the airport shuttle bus, driven by a large, plump, smiling Indian fellow in a yellow turban, made it's way through the streets of Edinburgh, Cameron basked in the sights. He just loved the whole place. The old sandstone buildings , the flower filled gardens , the Scottish people in their Scottish clothes – fashionable but conservative , the pubs with their fantastic names – "The Cauldron" , "The Deaf Dug" , "The Neep and Tatties"…. The sun was shining and Edinburgh looked very happy. The Captain of Singapore Airlines flight 202 had stated that it was 18 degrees centigrade at the airport when they had arrived. Fantastic. They had arrived in a heatwave. Mid July. Scottish people would be collapsing from heat stroke today – the hospitals would be full. Cameron had left the Blue Mountains in mid-winter where the temperatures were down to 24 degrees centigrade during the day and people were wearing hats and scarves… At 18 degrees in Edinburgh people were pouring out into the parks and sun-baking. It was a glorious day.

The bus crept passed Edinburgh Zoo. Cameron had had a wonderful time there as a child. His father had brought he and his brothers there when they were all still in primary school. It had been a great day out. They travelled by train and crossed the Forth Railway Bridge before arriving in central Edinburgh and getting on an old bus to the zoo. They had spent the day looking at every animal that lived in the whole wide world - elephants, gorillas, monkeys, seals, penguins and more. It was the greatest day. Probably a day which forged the path that Cameron was going to follow for the next hundred years. He had loved animals before the visit. After the visit, he talked, read, dreamed and breathed animals. He was either going to be the next Jacques Cousteau or become a vet and work with animals every day. He still had clear memories of his dad talking to some large Amazonian parrots through the wires of a cage and the parrots managing to steal the lens cover off his small camera. He and his brothers had almost wet themselves laughing.

After the zoo, Murrayfield Stadium could be seen off to the right. Cameron could catch glimpses of the vast structure in the distance. Rows of neat and tidy sandstone houses lined the route now – some which advertised as "B and B's" with names like "The Scrummage" and "The Lineout". Murrayfield is the home of Scottish Rugby and Cameron had spent many happy days in and around Murrayfield. He'd been witness to great Scottish victories and tragic Scottish defeats there, but win or lose every Murrayfield visit ended with a mass exodus of singing fans migrating to Rose Street for celebration and revelry. He had enjoyed some of the most memorable days and weekends on visits to Murrayfield. He recalled being in a pub in Rose Street after a Scotland v Ireland match in the eighties. The place was absolutely packed and the noise and the singing was deafening. The entrance to the pub was a large glass revolving door. A young man wearing a kilt and holding a pint glass of frothing ale climbed onto the cover over the revolving door and proceeded to lead the singing and conduct the masses from this fantastic spot above the crowd. Suddenly the glass beneath his feet gave way and he disappeared through the roof of the door. The whole crowd gasped. Singing abruptly stopped. You could have heard a pin drop. No one could see the door through the crowd. Surely he must be dead. Seconds passed. The crowd stared towards the door... No sound at all. Then suddenly, a cry from the door – "he's alive". The whole pub erupted in an explosion of noise and for the next 10-15 minutes the massed Scottish and Irish voices sang "He's alive, He's alive, He's alive..." to the tune of one of their favourite anthems. A historic night. A legendary night...

Slowly the outskirts of town gave way to large sandstone tenement buildings with shops and businesses on the lower floors and flats in the storeys above. Shopping Malls filled some of these large red buildings. The traffic became very dense with traffic lights and pedestrian crossings slowing the bus's progress. As the bus entered "Haymarket" the bus stopped to deliver passengers to their hotels.

Most of the hotels looked very nice, The Haymarket Hotel, The Tune Hotel and The Leonardo Hotels all looked welcoming. Cameron had looked at all of these on the internet before deciding to book in to the Sheraton – the determining factor was that the Sheraton offered special deals to conference delegates and he thought that there were likely to be more chance of meeting up with old friends there because of this. He wondered if he'd made the right choice.

The bus pulled in to Festival Square and the driver announced "Sheraton Grand Hotel and Spa – next stop". As the bus pulled up outside the hotel several other passengers stood and stretched and made their way down the aisle of the bus. None looked like vets – but hey - what does a vet look like? There were no tweed jackets with leather elbows on this bus – but that fashion was only peculiar to UK vets – those which were brought up on James Herriot and Siegfried and Tristan Farnon. Vets from elsewhere in the world tended to be a lot more casual in appearance these days. The Japanese and American tourists old and young – disembarking here – looked just like Japanese and American tourists old and young... Cameras firing at every opportunity, constantly calling out to others in their group. These looked like real holiday makers.

Cameron climbed out of the bus and let the others fight over the baggage delivered onto the pavement by the bus driver. When the excitement was over he calmly lifted his case and strolled through the automatic glass entrance doors and into the foyer. Large comfortable sofas and pouffs were scattered around coffee tables strewn with newspapers and glossy magazines. The colours were cosy reds and browns matching the colours in the deep tartan carpet underfoot. The carpet gave way to a dark slate grey polished stone floor which led to two metallic reception desks. Although there were 5 receptionists, each was busy with new arrivals from Cameron's bus and another bus which had arrived minutes before. He joined the shortest queue and waited his turn. The walls of the lobby were adorned with pictures of Edinburgh castle, highland scenes and pictures of deer with huge antlers. Cameron wondered how many deer there were in Edinburgh these days. The décor was actually very nice and did deliver a feeling of being in a Scotland from bygone years with a modern twist in the comfortable furniture.

A nicely spoken Asian woman in dark tartan Sheraton Uniform welcomed Cameron to the Sheraton and asked if he had a reservation. He produced his booking reference and she punched her computer keyboard officiously and produced two plastic key cards for him. After taking a copy of his mastercard number and getting his signature in case he ran off without paying his bar fridge account, she told him that he was in room 444 – on the fourth floor looking out towards the castle, the lifts were off to his right, his baggage would be delivered to his room in a couple of minutes and she hoped that he would have a wonderful stay in Edinburgh. He smiled and thanked her and as he walked past the other receptionists at the desks who looked to be from all corners of the globe he wondered if there were actually any Scottish people working in Edinburgh.

The lift took him to the fourth floor. The brightly lit carpeted corridor led him to room 444. He inserted one of his key cards and then pushed door handle down. As he opened the door he was delighted with the room before him. Immediately to his left was a marble tiled bathroom – immaculate and shining - and the short hallway from the door opened onto a large bedroom with a huge double bed, a coffee table surrounded by comfortable armchairs and a sofa, and a small business table with phone and computer connection terminals against the same wall as the bed head. Windows took up the far wall and the curtains were open. The view was magnificent. Edinburgh Castle stood grandly on it's mountainous rock, filling most of the window. The sun was shining brightly and the sky was perfect blue. The view was stunning. The Sheraton Hotel and Spa was the best choice ever. He dropped his small back pack on the bed and crossed to the window.

Between the hotel and the castle he could see the domed roof of the Usher Hall, and the rooftops of other stunning sandstone buildings. He could see the traffic heading towards Castle Terrace and Kings Stable Road down Cambridge Road. To the right – he saw the rooftops of buildings to the south of the castle. Were they university buildings? Maybe his bearings were wrong. Or were they ancient school buildings? He knew that the school which JK Rowling had based Hogwarts School of Witchcraft and Wizardry on in the Harry Potter's novels lay out there somewhere… Couldn't see too many turrets and towers though. To the left he could see across to Princes Street over the top of Princes Street Gardens. He knew that Rose Street lay immediately behind. What a spot. Stunning. Cameron was delighted. He stood and stared for several minutes until there was a quiet knock on the room door.

A bell-boy had arrived with his case. He carried it into the room and deposited it on the suitcase stand. "Thank you", Cameron said. "My pleasure sir. If you need anything else just call reception. My name is Ramone and if I can be of any help at all just ring." The young man was slim and small with unblemished olive skin and jet black short greased hair. His smile was infectious. His accent Spanish? Maybe Portuguese?

Cameron held out his hand. "My name is Cameron – I'm originally from Scotland but now I live in Australia. Where are you from?" Ramone shook Cameron's hand enthusiastically. "I am from Madrid in Spain. I'm studying naval architecture at Edinburgh University. I am very pleased to meet you Mr Cameron. "

"Are you a football fan?"

"Everyone from Madrid is a football fan," he beamed.

Cameron laughed. "Here's the big question. Who is your team? Real or Atletico?"

He looked a little sheepish for a second or two and then a broad grin crept across his face.

"They are both very good teams but I actually support someone else..."

There was a very pregnant pause before he added, "I support the greatest team in the world... Barcelona..."

They both erupted in laughter.

Cameron grinned and enthused, "They are one of my favourite teams. Lionel Messi is a genius. Iniesta, Neymar, Suarez, Pique, Rakitic – they are all superb players. They play wonderful football. I have only one problem with them." The young Spaniard looked bemused. "What is this problem?"

"They beat my team – Glasgow Celtic 7-0 in the Champions League 2016."

Once again the pair roared in laughter. Ramone was smirking. His eyes sparkling. He stated, "I'm very sorry… We only beat you 2-0 in Glasgow…"

The laughter continued. Cameron asked, "My brothers are both Glasgow Rangers supporters and they always give me hell. What do your family say about you supporting Barcelona?"

"My father disowned me and my brothers took out a mafia contract on me… But they still love me and give me presents at Christmas…"

They both laughed a lot more and grinned at each other.

"Really nice to meet you Ramone. I will hopefully see you again while I'm here."

"Great to meet you Mr Cameron. Remember if you need anything at all please don't hesitate to ask for me in reception."

When Ramone left the room Cameron sat down on the bed and flicked on the TV. Sitting down was a big mistake. Suddenly he felt exhausted. The bed was too comfortable. If he shut his eyes he would be out like a light. The TV screen lit up with a list of channels to choose from but Cameron was taken by a message running along the bottom of the screen. "Welcome to the Sheraton Mr Woods. We hope you enjoy you're stay here. You have two messages left on your answer service. Please hit the green button on the remote to receive your messages."

Interesting… He hit the green button.

Two messages appeared in print across the screen of the wall mounted TV.

1. Hopefully catch you tonight at drinkees – Loges XX

2. Cameron – Looking forward to catching up with you in the next few days. Shona.

Cameron's heart jumped. Suddenly he was wide awake. The first message was good. That was from Logan Bloomsberry the man with the fattest arse in the world. He was here – hopefully with the missus and keen for a wee snort. Fantastic. The second message he read and re-read. Shona was looking forward to catching up. Repeat Shona was looking forward to catching up. He pictured her on a beach on the Costa-del-sol. Absolutely fantastic. Better than fantastic.

He lay back on the bed and pictured Shona Soutar in his mind's eye. The years had been kind to her. She still looked like she was just out of high school. Her skin beautiful. Her eyes twinkling. Her lips grinning from ear to ear when she spotted him in the crowd. Her boobs... Man they were still magnificent... He felt himself relaxing into the warmth of the bed clothes. God this was cosy... And Shona was beckoning him...

Suddenly his real brain kicked in. If he stayed on the bed he wasn't going to meet anyone at drinkees tonight. He was probably going to sleep for a day and a half. He forced himself up from the bed and slouched into the bathroom. He looked at the haggard looking man in the mirror. Grey two day stubble, black sunken eyes and dirty wrinkled clothes.

"Looking real sexy Cam... Time for a long cold shower..."

Chapter 5

A long cold shower and two mugs of strong black instant coffee didn't really revive Cameron. The good news however was that he was still awake and on course to get to opening night drinks at the conference. He dressed smart, but casual. No need for a collar and tie tonight. He chose comfortable boat shoes, cream pants and a long sleeved paisley patterned shirt in blues and mauves. He loved shirts and this was one of his very favourites. He didn't want to dress too loudly but wanted to be quietly sexy and add the subtle hint of a bohemian lurking underneath his business like exterior. The shave had removed the silver stubble from his chin. This was actually a shame he thought as silver went well with the mauve in the shirt. Ah well. The black holes around his eyes had no suggestion of any bohemian at all – unless of one who had been on a 3 day bender.

He squirted on enough aftershave to be smelled easily up the M8 in Glasgow and gelled his hair into small ruffled spikes. For some reason he kept hearing guitar riffs from Duran Duran and Spandau Ballet songs.

A glance at his phone. Five pm Edinburgh time. Official opening time at the conference was 6 pm. If he sat down he'd fall asleep. He decided to head out and wander slowly to the conference centre and take in the Edinburgh sights along the way. It looked like a beautiful evening outside.

Maybe he should phone home – let Alison know that he'd arrived safely. The idea didn't excite him. He checked the world clock in his phone. Five pm Edinburgh – 4 am Australian Eastern... He'd be popular if he phoned now. He filed the thought in the "To do Later" basket.

In the foyer Cameron stopped to talk to the Concierge about the route to the Edinburgh International Conference Centre and was given a small map and nice concise instructions as to how to get there and the sights he should take in on the way. He spotted Ramone pushing a trolley of suitcases for several young Japanese ladies and beaming from ear to ear.

Ramone waved and called, "Have a nice night Mr Cameron."

"You too Ramone – and don't work too hard..." he called back.

He passed through the sliding glass doors into the early evening sunshine on the castle side of the hotel. The sky was blue and cloudless. There was the slightest hint of a breeze. He estimated the temperature to be 22 degrees..ish... It was an absolutely prefect evening.

The castle stood majestically above Edinburgh on it's huge basalt throne. The Usher Hall with it's green domed roof and yellow-brown sandstone walls rose from street level a hundred metres in front of him, between the hotel and the castle. The hall was a very impressive building in it's own right, but sitting below the castle, you could be forgiven for glancing at it only for a moment. The castle was magnificent. Cameron stood for several minutes on the hotel forecourt and just stared at the castle. He loved it. He'd had many visits there in his childhood. He loved the crown jewels, the one o'clock cannon shot from the turrets, the ancient dog's cemetery – for soldiers' dogs, the weaponry, the dungeons, the centuries of history, the myths, the ghosts, the legends, the amazing views over the city and the sheer beauty. He remembered that only 4 or 5 years ago he had attended the Edinburgh Military Tattoo with Alison and his mum and dad. The Tattoo is held in a stadium that is erected from huge scaffolding structures on the forecourt of the castle every August/September. The stadium had stood at the top of the royal mile on the opposite side of the castle from his present vantage point. It had been a great night. Marching military bands from all corners of the globe played rousing marching music and national anthems, and off course The Royal Scots Dragoons Guards brought the house down playing "Amazing Grace" and "Scotland the Brave". It was a stunning show – completed with a fantastic firework and laser show. Mum and Dad had loved it, Alison had been thrilled to bits. Unfortunately his Dad was a tight-arse and would not pay money to stay in a hotel or motel, and at 10 o'clock at night, Cameron had to drive his hire car 3 hours back to Aberdeen while everybody else snored their heads off. A fantastic day... He loved the castle.

He stepped down onto the lawn and sauntered across the grass towards Lothian Road. There were groups of oriental tourists photographing each other and taking selfies with the Sheraton in the background, and also the Usher hall in the background, and of course with the castle in the background. Young couples sat on the grass and canoodled and drank from champagne glasses. Others simply lay on the grass and enjoyed the gorgeous sunshine. A small black hairy dog ran around chasing pigeons back into the sky where they belonged.

Once on the pavement at Lothian Road he veered right and wandered past The Edinburgh Filmhouse where patrons spilled onto the pavement enjoying pre movie drinks and nibbles. Between the Filmhouse and the Lothian Street / Morrison Street junction restaurant goers sat out on the pavement eating Italian and Indian food. The food looked delicious and the smells were wonderful. Cameron realised it was a long time since he'd had a decent meal and started paying close attention to the menu boards outside the restaurants. He thought that one Italian restaurant might have been playing a bit too much towards the tourist crowd… It's menu included "Haggis Frittata" and "Neep and Tattie Bolognaise". Bizarre…but Cameron was salivating. The good news was there were no deep fried Mars Bars to be seen.

He turned right into Morrison Street and continued to pass nice eateries with the hubbub of conversation, the clinking of glasses and the aromas of beautiful foods filling the air. He stopped outside a busy fish restaurant called "Jonah's" and read the menu. It looked divine – seared scallops with beetroot and pastis, lobster with lime butter and coriander, salmon coulibiac – salmon and wild mushrooms baked in a pastry case, grilled flounder with herb butter and quinoa… My God it looked better than fantastic… He was lost deep in thought tasting every dish on the menu inside his head when suddenly he felt a stinging smack in the middle of his back and his ears exploded as a voice shouted directly into his ear. He must have jumped several inches in the air. As he turned warily and prepared himself to fend off whoever this crazy assailant was he looked straight into the laughing face of Logan Bloomsberry. His face was creased in laughter and there were tears in the corners of his eyes.

"Cambo you bastard..." he was still shouting extremely loudly, "We were hoping we'd bump into you." He flung his arms around Cameron and engulfed him in a giant bear hug. Cameron, finally recognising his old uni mate, now grinned from ear to ear. As he was released from the long hug, he grabbed his friends face, pulled it down to his level and planted a large wet kiss on his cheek.

"You scared the Bejesus out of me you lard-arsed prick."

Logan laughed, "God you were always a girl...Good to see nothing's changed."

Logan had Cameron by the arm and was leading him into the restaurant, weaving between tables and bemused waiters. They stopped at a small table in the middle of the room where a blonde goddess stood up and gently wrapped her arms around Cameron and hugged him warmly. Cameron melted into the hug. This was one of his favourite women in the whole universe. Electra Bloomsberry nee Von Humberg. Cameron loved this woman. She was simply gorgeous. He thought she was the most beautiful creature on the planet. She was blonde, with striking blue eyes and Scandinavian skin – smooth and blemish free. She was slim but curvaceous... Most importantly she was married to one of his best friends and had nursed him through some very difficult times lately. He loved her like a sister.

Cameron was absolutely delighted. Logan had been very tall and handsome back in the day. He'd had a mop of blonde hair, twinkling blue eyes and a poncy English accent. Women had thrown themselves at him. God only knew why. His arse was bigger than Ben Hur but the women didn't seem to notice that. After uni he'd worked in equine practice for only 2 years before moving into pharmaceuticals. Twenty or so years ago he had moved to Denmark to take up a post with "Fleuchters Pharma", an up and coming pharmaceutical company based in Copenhagen. The company since then had become a squillion dollar multi-national company with laboratories and factories all over the world. Logan had risen through the company ranks quickly and easily and now was on the Board of Directors and owned a healthy slice of the huge business. He was now managing a territory which extended across the whole of Europe and into Northern Africa.

Soon after moving to Denmark, Logan had married the beautiful Electra. She was a distant relative of the Danish Royal family. Their wedding had been huge and Cameron had been flown to Copenhagen from Australia to be Logan's Best Man. The celebrations were fantastic and Cameron's recollection of events had always been clouded in an alcoholic blur. He knew he'd had a great time, but couldn't remember many details.

Logan and Electra had 2 beautiful daughters and a handsome son. The girls, Isabella and Anna, were studying at Swedish universities – both studying medicine. Christian - the baby - was studying chemical engineering at Harvard in the US.

As Cameron sat at the table and listened to Logan laughing and recounting stories of the good old days, he studied his friend. He had worn a lot in the last couple of years. His hairline had receded and the remaining straggly silver hair was thin and sparse on top. His skin was pale and paper like. He had lost at least 30 kg. The big arse was just not what it used to be. Cancer was a cruel thing. Logan had undergone 2 major surgeries in the last 18 months. Bowel cancer had resulted in the loss of much of his small intestine and part of his stomach. Chemotherapy had ravaged his body further, but the good news was that he was still here and still exuded a great Joi de Vie.

Electra was as stunning as ever but she looked tired. He knew she had lived every minute of Logan's treatment with him. He knew her energy levels were low. He knew she worried. He understood. How on earth could she not worry?

He was delighted to see them. He ordered champagne and the Salmon Coulibiac. They were ready for desserts, but postponed so that he could eat with them and they could talk quietly before being swamped by old friends and vet talk at the conference.

When Logan asked how Alison was, both he and Electra understood that things were far from right. They understood despite his forced enthusiasm and his joking descriptions of her reasons for staying behind. They understood more from the things he didn't say than from the things he did say. Although Cameron laughed about her absence and how he wished she were here – his body language and his hurt eyes told a very different story. Logan and Electra both kindly took the conversation elsewhere.

The dessert menu was fantastic. Both Logan and Electra chose liqueur sorbets and local berries and Cameron chose the cheese platter. He reckoned that if the champagne kept coming at same rate as the last 2 bottles he needed something substantial to soak it up. The cheeses were divine, accompanied by oatcakes and fruit. Just what the doctor ordered.

As Cameron picked through the last small fragments of oatcake Logan raised his champagne glass and stated, "I'd like to make a toast."

Both Electra and Cameron raised their glasses in anticipation.

"To absent friends."

Their eyes met over the top of clinking champagne flutes. They stared at each other. The moment was fleeting but lasted an age, each sad in their own thoughts but trying to read the others.

"To Damien…," Logan added quietly.

They each sipped champagne and continued to stare at each other.

"Did anyone see it coming?" asked Cameron.

"Nobody that we've talked to", stated Logan now staring absently at his crumpled serviette. He continued, "Such an absolute waste. One of the world's true gentlemen… A very gentle man…"

"How was the funeral?" Cameron asked.

"Terribly sad… Lydia was a mess. She looked terrible. The kids held her up all the way. The flowers and the cask were beautiful. I hear Randal and Harold picked up the tab for the whole thing… You probably know – he'd recently sold his practice to Noah's Ark and had been working for them for several months… All the rugby boys were there except you and William. He was in Belfast having more chemotherapy. It was an extremely quiet affair. Most people didn't stay for the wake. The few of us that did – Peter and Claire, Gregor and Jacqui, Mick, Shona,

Harry and Randal, and a few relatives only - had a very quiet shandy and left mid-afternoon – It was a one o'clock service... Lydia was almost hysterical despite heavy sedation. The kids did their best to be sociable but none of them could talk for long without getting emotional and falling apart. It really was a terrible day. Not the celebration of a life. More an accentuation of grief and despair..."

All three sat at the table and quietly stared at nothing in particular.

Eventually Cameron asked, "Does anyone have any idea why he did it?"

Logan shook his head slowly and Electra continued to stare at her champagne glass. She had tears rolling down her cheeks.

"The story I got was that he hanged himself in his office. The local papers said only that he had passed away. Do we know what happened? Was he ill? Was all well with him and Lydia? Were his kids all behaving?"

No Answers came. Logan quietly stood up and came round the table and bent over Cameron. Once again, he wrapped Cameron in a huge bear hug. Electra joined her husband and Cameron was held in a stifling group hug for the best part of a minute.

Suddenly, Logan released his grip and his booming voice cried out. "Come on. Let's go and get pissed on conference champagne."

Chapter 6

They walked out of the restaurant hand in hand, Electra a beautiful rose between two thorns. Logan and Electra were chattering about the wonderful food and wine they'd just enjoyed but Cameron was on a different wavelength.

In his mind he saw Damien Corrigan. Five feet nothing with thick black hair growing out of every part of his body except his eyeballs and dense brown freckles on every piece of skin without hair. He was always smiling or grinning. He was the best fly half the uni had ever seen. His rugby shirt dwarfed him and he played with the sleeves rolled up and the bottom of his shirt hanging around his knees. Dave had married Lydia a vet nurse at the practice where he got his first job, straight out of uni. The practice was in Everton, Liverpool. Dave was born and bred on Norris Green Estate in Liverpool and was a Liverpool FC supporter from birth. When he started work in the suburb of Everton he felt like a traitor working in the homeland of Everton FC - Liverpool FC's bitter rivals. He managed to get his head around this turn of events by telling himself it was great to take money from Everton supporters rather than Liverpool supporters. The practice had been a very small business, owned by an elderly vet called Graham Shankley. He wanted to work less and eventually sell the practice. This suited Damien to a tee and he became the practice owner within 5 years of being employed. He then grew the practice into a 5 vet Small Animal Practice and built a state of the art hospital facility over the next 20 years. Lydia and he got married quietly in 1989 and had three children over the next 8 years – Jane, Jessica and James. Cameron had received photos of babies and birthdays and holidays every Xmas since. Damien and Lydia had visited Cameron and Alison in the Blue Mountains the year after they married and boasted that Jane was conceived after a long day exploring the Jenolan Caves... Cameron had suggested that maybe she was conceived during the half hour that Damien and Lydia had spent in one of the caves on their own while Cameron and Alison had sought fluid therapy in the Hotel above. He'd met the kids on a couple of UK visits over the years and loved them dearly. They called him "Uncle Cambo". Lydia was the girl next door - pretty, no nonsense, with a great sense of humour. She could be very caustic when pissed off. She loved Damien and the kids unconditionally. She had worked in the practice intermittently while the kids were growing up and had returned in a practice management role when the kids had all gone to uni. She was a qualified nurse trainer and a strong political voice in the Royal Animal Nursing Auxiliary. She was listed as a speaker in the "Nurses Stream" at the Edinburgh Conference.

The sale of Damien's beloved practice to Noah's Ark Veterinary Hospitals came as a bit of a surprise to Cameron but he understood that if no succession plan was in place then these corporate groups would often pay a very good price for a practice allowing a senior veterinarian to retire without the worry of hoping to sell to other partners or employees. Once sold the seller was often encouraged to work on in the practice for a couple of years for a salary and provide continuity. In Australia this type of sale had been happening for several years, but most private practice vets tended to treat the corporate groups as sharks...buying practices from older vets who had no succession plan and then becoming big players in the veterinary market controlling multiple practices and wielding power to buy drugs and equipment in bulk. This cut costs which other private practices could not do. They had the reputation that drug wholesalers would kow-tow to their wishes because of their buying power and the threat that they could take their business elsewhere. Once the practice was sold, corporate protocols then dictated how the practice was run – from staff employment through to which vaccines to use and protocols for treatment of different diseases. Many who had sold to the corporate groups had not stayed to work for the years they had promised, as they could not stand watching their practice being run by "money-men" who seemed to have no interest in animal or staff welfare. Profit seemed to be their most important aim. Cameron was sure there had to be good corporate groups out there... but he was extremely wary.

He had assumed that Damien was setting up to retire happily. He would have received a very nice nest egg from NAVHs. Then why on earth did he hang himself? The horrible vision of his friend hanging by the neck from a beam in his office ceiling crept into his mind's eye. The vision had haunted him for months. The detail got worse every time. Damien's face was blue and horrifically distorted. His eyes were empty – huge glassy dilated pupils. They stared vacantly. Saliva and frothy blood stained his black lips and filled his silently screaming mouth. His body hung limply below the rope which had tightened into a deep furrow in his neck and small dribbles of blood and serum oozed from bruised skin under the noose. His clothes were dishevelled. His trousers stained with urine and faeces... His feet suspended above dirty wet stains on the floor...

"Cambo, Cambo...Are you OK buddy?" Logan Bloomsberry was holding either side of Cameron's face and talking to him from only inches away.

"Sorry Loges – I was miles away... Must be the Jet lag..."

"We thought you were going to fall into the traffic big boy. Too much champagne?"

"Are you OK Cameron?" Electra's beautiful Scandinavian accent brought him right back into the real world.

He smiled sheepishly. "Sorry...I was just miles away."

"The good news is that the conference centre is only about one minute walk from here and we'll be there in a skip, hop and a run..." Electra beamed at him.

"Darling I think you mean – a hop, skip and a jump..." said Logan.

"Bloody foreigners," stated Cameron shaking his head slowly. They all laughed and continued their walk along the busy pavement.

Chapter 7

Morrison Street was very busy. It had to be well after 6pm by now. There were people out jogging and dog walking. There were people enjoying meals on the street outside more restaurants. The traffic on the road was intense and chaotic. The sun was still high in a cloudless sky and shining brightly. The hint of a breeze cooled the sun-drenched pedestrians. Cameron and his two friends wandered slowly along the pavement.

As they walked past the Law Society of Scotland building the Edinburgh International Conference Centre appeared ahead on their right. The building was impressive. Concrete and glass rising 4-5 storeys from the pavement with a huge circular glass and concrete structure sitting high above the main building. Huge brightly coloured banners stretching from the pavement to the third and fourth floor windows announced "Welcome to WSAVA Conference Edinburgh 2017".

They entered the building via glass doors which opened directly onto Morrison Street and followed a steady trickle of people into the beautiful atrium. Banners on walls, laser lights from the ceiling and huge video screens welcomed veterinarians from all corners of the globe to the beautiful city of Edinburgh for the WSAVA conference. Scottish country dance music filled the air. They joined the queue at the well manned registration desk and were soon signed in and wearing lanyards announcing them as paid up delegates and carrying small backpacks filled with conference programs, free gifts from drug companies and tickets for various dinners and breakfasts that they had been invited to during the upcoming week. Once signed in they followed the movement of other newly arrived delegates and entered the Strathblane Hall.

The hall was packed from wall to wall with chatting, hugging, hand shaking delegates. There were groups of new graduates dressed casually in shorts and T-shirts and summer frocks. Older delegates were dressed from casual to very formal, jeans and short sleeved shirts, through to Tweed jackets with leather elbows and matching tweed ties, to three piece suits and cocktail dresses. Learned academics were present sporting bow-ties and haircuts that went out 30 years ago – already expounding to the masses the wonders of their latest break-throughs. The exhibition stalls set up by pharmaceutical companies, medical equipment companies, veterinary insurance companies and every other man and his dog stretched to all corners of the hall. The noise of happy chat, laughter and clinking glasses filled the air. Logan accosted a passing waitress in a blue tartan dress and collected three glasses of bubbly. Electra, Logan and Cameron toasted each other – "To a fantastic week," shouted Logan above the hubbub. They all grinned and skulled the champagne.

"Mmm... that's rather nice," stated Electra beaming. "We'd better find some more."

As if by magic another tartan clad waitress appeared on Cameron's shoulder and presented them with three more glasses of bubbles. This was going to be a good evening.

Out of nowhere a large round, red faced man wearing a green velvet jacket and matching bow tie bounced into their midst. He almost fell over in the process but skilfully managed to hold onto a pint of lager in each hand without spilling a single drop. Peter McEwan's grin stretched from ear to ear. His loud Glaswegian voice boomed.

"Welcome back to the motherland lads and lass. It's absolutely brilliant you made it."

Peter wrapped his arms around Cameron and hugged him warmly. Cameron felt the lovely sensation of ice cold lager dribbling down the back of his shirt. He released Cameron and repeated the hug on both Logan and Electra.

"Great to see you Petey," cried Logan. "You're looking great. Nice outfit."

Peter didn't see the sarcasm at all. "Thanks Loges – picked it up on ma last wee trip to Italy. In Milan – they know a thing or two about fashion there... I'll get you their e-mail address... All they need is your measurements. Cheers – great to see you all." Peter took a long sup on one of his pints.

Cameron grinned. "Great to see you Peter. You're looking well. How are the girls? Is Claire here?"

"Aye – My gorgeous wee Clairey's doon the middle there somewhere talking to Harry at the Noah's Ark stand. I had to escape. Canna stand that corporate evangelical bullshit... I know their doing well but no need to force it doon everybuddy else's throats.... The girls are great – costing me a fortune but they're just the best." The warmth which oozed out of Peter when he talked about his girls could melt anyone's heart. He beamed. "Evie's in Rome doing her PhD in fine art, Bernadette is still in New York running an art gallery and dating Jerome Rearden who plays basketball for the Jets, Maria is in Law School in Edinburgh here and Madonna plays second violin in the Scottish Philharmonic Orchestra and is currently in Barcelona on a concert tour. They're all unmarried. Madonna is dating a Japanese bassoonist and Maria is dating her professor... I think Evie might be batting for the other team – but hey - one carpet muncher out of four is not bad heh?"

As Cameron exploded with laughter champagne bubbles and froth shot out of his nose and he coughed and choked. He struggled to get his breath for several seconds. When he had recomposed and mopped his face with a napkin he looked at Peter and smiled, "That's great Pete – give my love to them all when you talk to them next."

Cameron looked at his old friend. He had aged dramatically since their last meeting. Cameron wondered how other people would see him this trip. Had he aged like Peter? Did he look as unhealthy? Was he the same person that went to uni all those years ago or had time and life changed him for ever?

Peter's taste in clothes had not changed. His love of life had not changed. His love of alcohol appeared undiminished. His hair was thinning and silver grey. His red face and his expanded waistline made him look like a heart attack waiting to happen. Pete had married Cozette Bunyan. She was a very attractive girl at vet school two years below the class of '85. Her first job out of uni was at the practice Pete was working at in

Inverness. They fell in love, married, had four daughters and stayed married for the best part of twenty years. Cozette was high maintenance throughout their married life but as the years passed she suffered from mental problems and became more and more psychotic. She would disappear from home for days on end. She became hyper religious. Prayer meetings with other religious nutters would happen at the McEwan home when Pete was out working hard. Cozette started donating large amounts of money to her church. She started drinking heavily and beating the girls. She also beat Peter on several occasions. Peter threw her out when he came home early one day and found her shagging the plumber on the kitchen floor. Finding his wife shagging a hairy fat plumber was bad enough, but the tattoo on his arse was too much… "Rangers for Ever". Generations of Peter's family were devout Celtic supporters. Enough was enough. There was no coming back from there. Pete was now happily married to Claire – a nurse at his Inverness practice for fifteen years. All the rugby boys thought that Pete was now very happy and the best news was that the kids all loved his new wife. The settlement was excruciating – especially as Peter had to pay for Cozette's mental health bills throughout.

Cameron looked at is friend. You look like shit Peter but… you are happy… I think you're happy… you have a loving wife and four loving daughters…

Logan pushed another champagne glass into his hand as Pete led them through the throng towards where he had left his lovely wife. As they moved between the exhibition stalls the dense crowd of delegates made it difficult for Cameron to keep up. He was in no hurry though – he scanned the crowd for familiar faces as he slowly moved towards the centre of the hall. He'd been in Australia so long that he actually knew very few of the veterinary graduates of the last twenty years. There were reunions going on all around him. Delegates were hugging, laughing and sharing stories of weddings, births, veterinary achievements and of course veterinary disasters. He was enjoying the atmosphere moving slowly through the masses when he felt a tug on his arm.

He turned to find a grinning Jacqui Alcott throwing her arms around him and engulfing him in a long hug. She squeezed tightly against him and held him for several seconds her head nuzzling into the side of his face. She eventually relaxed her hold but did not let go. She pulled her head around to look straight into Cameron's face from only a couple of inches away. She looked great. A shaggy perm with blonde highlights in chocolate brown hair cascading over her shoulders. Skin smooth and lightly tanned with very fine crow's feet at the edges of her eyes. Her eyes – alive and twinkling, dark brown irises and long lashes. Her lips full and moist with stunningly white teeth a little too large for her mouth. She smelled divine… Roses and gardenia Cameron thought… Just like back in the old days. She didn't move away. He could feel the warmth of her boobs pushing into his chest and the warmth of her stomach pushed against his. He felt a stirring in his groin.

"I'm so glad you're here Cambo…It's just great to see you. You look fantastic."

"You're looking rather fantastic yourself Jacqui… You still look thirty years old. "

She beamed and hugged him closer again.

When she leaned back to look him in the face again she said, "I hear you're travelling on your own?"

Cameron nodded, "Yes… Alison had other commitments this time round."

"That's a shame… Gregor couldn't come either…"

She continued grinning and looked him straight in the eye. "We'll need to do dinner and have a few drinks one night this week…"

"That would be wonderful," Cameron enthused… While one half of his brain screamed at him – "She's off her fucking head you muppet," the other half tried to control the erection that was suddenly growing in his underpants. He tried to subtly move is groin further from Jacqui's but the lower half of her body followed his and ground against him. They stood entwined staring at each other for several seconds while the crowd ebbed and flowed round about them.

Suddenly a deep gravelly Irish voice boomed in their ears, "Can anybody join in this game?" At the same instant the huge figure of William P O'Shaunessy wrapped the pair of them in a monster hug and tried to lift them off the floor. As he released them they pulled apart and both Jacqui and Cameron hugged William individually. Cameron dropped a hand into his trouser pocket to make sure his huge stiffy did not make any contact at all with the big man as he hugged him – Fuck wouldn't that be nice way to say hello...

"Great to see you Jacqui," stated the legendary rugby captain, "And Cameron it's an absolute pleasure to see you again. How long has it been? Ten? Twelve years? Way too long. You look great. You both look great."

"It's so good to be here," Cameron replied. "You look fantastic. How are you travelling?"

"Can't complain. Nobody would listen anyway. The missus still gives me a feed and half a bed every night. The kids are have all flown the coup. What more could you ask for?"

Cameron looked at William while he continued to expound the wonderful state of the whole world without actually saying anything that meant much. William had suffered from a bizarre form of cancer for the last fifteen or sixteen years which had affected the nerves to his lower limbs. He had undergone multiple surgeries and numerous rounds of chemotherapy. He could still walk with the aid of a stick but both his legs had withered and his coordination was not good at all. He was very shy about talking about his health problems. None of the boys knew the specific diagnosis but it was understood that he was likely to lose the use of his legs completely in time. The latest news on the grapevine was that a tumour had been detected in his lungs in the last 3 months and the prognosis was now even worse. Although William was still a very large man, he now walked with a stoop and was as skinny as a hat rack. He had no hair at all and his skin was pale and blotchy. Cameron went over and over in his head the fact that he had just told William he looked fantastic. He knew William wouldn't mind at all. Both Cameron and William knew that William looked far from fantastic. Cameron felt numb and wanted to rewind the tape and say something different. It wasn't going to happen.

William beamed at Cameron and Jacqui. "Now I've misplaced my stick somewhere between here and Harry's stand. I might need a wee help back to the missus. Jacqui – can you walk in front and part the masses while Cambo here gives me a shoulder to lean on?"

"Of course Willy," Jacqui announced, "I'll just tell them there's a drunk Irishman coming through..."

Jacqui turned and started gently making a path for them to follow. Cameron tucked himself under William's right arm and supported him as he walked. William waved to, and had a greeting for many of the delegates who moved to allow them to pass. Cameron's eyes followed Jacqui's delicious arse as it weaved through the crowd. My God she was still a stunning woman. He was hypnotised.

William's voice talked quietly into his ear as they followed the hypnotic derrière.

"Hey Cambo... Here's a wee bit of advice from Uncle Willy... Leave her alone..."he was staring at Jacqui's rear end also. "She's poison buddy. She's as mad as a meat axe."

Chapter 8

Jacqui's arse stopped just in front of the "Noah's Ark Veterinary Hospitals" stand. The floor in front of the stand was packed and delegates were listening to Harry Ainsley extolling the virtues of being a part of the greatest veterinary practice cooperative in Europe…..He was dressed in a three piece green tartan suit (odd for an Englishman), his hair was the stunning blond of his youth, his teeth were way whiter and straighter than Cameron remembered and his blemish free tanned skin had no wrinkles or creases at all. He looked great. His performance was mesmerising. He strutted backwards and forwards on the raised floor of the stand. The crowd followed his every move, drank in his every word. Harry reminded Cameron of James Brown. The stage show was very similar. He whispered to the audience – they strained to hear. He spoke louder and individuals in the crowd nodded in agreement with his words. As his voice rose to a crescendo and he announced "We will look after the best interests of all our employees and help them reach standards of veterinary medicine and surgery that they would never have dreamed of on their own. Anyone here can be a Noah's Ark employee. We would love you to join us. We will look after you during your working life and will help you reap the benefits of your work and make sure that when the time comes you can retire happily and comfortably and know that the high standards of your work will be carried on beyond your tenure." There was clapping and cheering and Harry waved to the masses. He finally stepped from the stage being engulfed by delegates desperate to make themselves known to him.

Big William leaned in to Cameron's ear, "I think U2 are on next."

They both laughed out loud and within a few moments Logan appeared through the crowd followed by an entourage of familiar faces and waitresses carrying trays of drinks and canapes.

"Thought we'd lost you," he laughed as he shoved a cold pint of lager into Cameron's hand.

Mick O'Reilly threw an arm around Cameron's shoulders and stuck a sticky wet kiss in his ear. "Great to see you big boy," he announced.

"Great to see you Mickus,"replied Cameron. "How're you going? Is Mandy here?"

Mick had been hooker in the rugby team back in the day. Short and squat and powerful. Now despite a rather large girth he still looked short and squat and powerful. The number one clip over his whole scalp emphasized the fact that he had little or no hair left. His blue eyes twinkled as they had done thirty years before. Mick was one of those hyper intelligent beings whose brain functions at levels that most people cannot even dream about. He had, however, been educated in a private boy's school in Northern Ireland where there was no contact with anything at all which was vaguely of the feminine gender. Once at uni, his superhuman brain was not stretched to the limit for the benefit of humankind - instead he stretched it beyond imagination trying to get any girl at all to go to bed with him. He was the loveliest guy but had been brought up with no social skills related to talking to girls, romance or femininity. As a result he spent his first three years at uni trying to work out in his head how you got a girl into bed. While everyone else around him was shagging like mad it drove him nuts. He would have shagged a hole in the wall if you let him, his frustrations were so immense. Eventually he encountered a nymphomaniac arts student who was as socially inept and as frustrated as him. They shagged for months on end before eventually remembering that they were at uni to study and returned to classes to fulfil their prior commitments. When Mick found the love of his life in bed with another girl one day he thought all his Christmas's had come at once. Unfortunately, the new girlfriend was only into girls and gave Mick a hiding when he tried to join the party. Mick's first serious relationship came to an abrupt halt right about then. The boys thought he would be heartbroken, but he moved on unfazed. After uni he moved back to Ireland to work in his father's practice in Armagh in the north. The practice ran on TB and Brucellosis testing back then but had now progressed to become a very high quality mixed practice employing five vets. Mick's Dad had retired ten years ago and Mick was now the sole owner. Mick had married Mandy , a hairdresser in town, two years after moving back to Ireland and had been happily married ever since. They had 5 children, all who now lived within twenty minutes of Mick and Mandy's home. Mick and Mandy were the first in Cameron's close group of friends to become grandparents. As far as Cameron was aware Mick hadn't shagged a hole in the wall for a couple of decades but there was always that worrying glimmer of excitement in his eyes when he had a few beers on board.

Mandy appeared over Mick's shoulder with Claire, Peter's wife, in tow. They both looked flushed and were giggling wildly. Mandy was small and matronly, had short black hair, wore minimal makeup and was dressed in a conservative black dress. Claire was tall and blonde with long flowing wavy hair. She was made up like she was on a model shoot and had a loud flowery dress with a plunging neckline revealing a very enticing cleavage. Long stiletto heels lifted her head and shoulders above Mandy.

Cameron let Mick go and hugged both Mandy and Claire.

"It is so good to see you guys here," he enthused. He smiled at them both and gave them each another hug to emphasise the fact.

"Great to see you Cameron," Mandy said, "I just wish you weren't on your own."

Claire nodded her agreement and squeezed his hand.

"Ah well – these things happen," he stated. "How did you enjoy the Harry Ainsley show?"

"We're assured by the man himself that there's a lot more to come." Claire joined in, "Did you know that he's a major sponsor here and he's a paid speaker too...in the practice management stream. He's talking about "Looking after your Hard Earned Cash" and "Making a succession plan"...All things that you, Peter and Mick should be thinking about..."

Mick took a long draw on his beer and chimed in, "I'm not selling my practice to that wanker so that he can make another million. Look where it left poor Damien...God bless his soul..."

Cameron thought it was about time to change tack and asked, "So is Randal here?"

Mick replied, "No – he's got bigger fish to fry... I hear he's in Geneva talking to the Swiss Veterinary Association about a liaison..."

"Wow – that's pretty interesting," mused Cameron.

"Aye. I think the pair of them would sell their mothers for a quid. It's all about getting stinking rich for them both. No ethics or morals there."

Logan joined in, "I thought I saw Belinda... the finance chick on the stage when we arrived. I thought she was bonking Randal. A bit odd he's off in Geneva and she's hanging about sunny Edinburgh with Tartan Harry..."

"She's a hard bitch. I think Harry and Randal have the ideas but she's the one that puts the hard word on people about the financial viability of their practice and what it's really worth to buy. She also puts the screws on the practices and makes sure they stick to protocols and only buy from NAVH's suppliers. I don't know where she came from – probably the Mafia or the Third Reich. I have absolutely no idea what Randal sees in her. She's stunning to look at – if you like Botox and fake boobs, but she's a soulless bitch. A robot. No feelings at all." Mick's latest comments left the little group wondering where to go next.

Logan piped in with a recurring favourite. "Time for more drinkees," he shouted at the top of his voice and within seconds tartan clad waitresses were offering trays of icy cold beer and champagne. Cameron collected another lager in his spare hand. He then gently wandered passed Mick and gave him a gentle nudge on the shoulder as he passed. He stood pretending to look at the merchandising and brochures on the NAVH's stall when Mick pulled up alongside. Without looking directly at him he said, "I'm missing something Mick. What's the tie in with Damien and NAVH's?"

Mick composed himself for a few seconds and then spoke quietly.

"Damien had sold to NAVH's about 12 months before he died. He had no up and coming partners to sell to and they gave him a reasonable price. Fine. But Damien said he'd work on for two or three years to give continuity and just so that he could earn an income before he really wanted to stop work all together. All went smoothly at first but when Dave bought products from reps who had become friends over the years the wheels started to fall off. These reps provided products that were not available elsewhere, but they were not in league with NAVHs, so the purchases were very much frowned upon. Damien was told to buy them out of his own pocket or not buy them at all. He did a lot of work for bird sanctuaries and welfare groups. He was instructed to bill them as normal clients and not to bill them for drugs only, or for cheaper than normal consultations. NAVHs were paying his salary and they weren't paying him to lose money for them... It wore on and on. Both Harry and Randal paid several visits to "smooth things out". Eventually Belinda started docking money out of Damien's salary. Damien was extremely unimpressed. The practice was still making a motza and he was being treated like shit. He phoned me and we discussed this on several occasions. He was going to take matters to the British Small Animal Veterinary Association and politicise what was happening. There were non-veterinarians involved dictating practice policy to him and agreed salary payments were not being met. He was going to visit the BSAVA president. Harry visited Damien the day before his appointment with the president. Damien committed suicide that very night."

Mick had started shaking. He was white and there were tears in his eyes.

"Jesus Christ," stammered Cameron..."Jesus Christ..."He stared unseeing at The NAHVs logo and the brightly coloured banners which covered the stall in front of them, the banners and the merchandising with happy veterinarians wearing stethoscopes and holding fluffy puppies and kittens. He was numb. He had been numb when he had found out that Damien had taken his own life. He was now completely blown away. He had just discovered the final push that sent him over the edge.

Mick wrapped an arm around his shoulder and shuffled him away from the stall. They wandered unspeaking through the crowd until they reached an empty sofa at the very edge of the hall. They sat quietly.

Mick finally spoke, "I can't bring myself to say a good word about Harry and Randal at the minute. Maybe they genuinely tried to sort things out but I can't believe they tried hard enough. Damien was a mate. A gentleman – he had more compassion and empathy in his little finger than the two of them put together. And now... They just trundle on doing the same thing. You saw Harry in action... He's a con man. Randal... We used to be close... He's lost the plot. He's shagging that fucking monster of a woman... He left his wife and kids for her... for this shit. He's a squillionaire... Who fucking cares. They've sold their souls."

Cameron was speechless. He could find nothing to say. He felt excruciatingly tired.

Chapter 9

Cameron and Mick supped lager quietly and watched the world go past. The sofa was comfortable. They relaxed. The delegates were of all sizes and shapes. Some of the older graduates looked great – fit looking, slim and well dressed. Others looked more like Michelin men with layers of middle-aged spread cascading over each other. Some had double chins, some had no chins at all. Some had hair, some had none, some had hair dyed all colours of the rainbow. Most were dressed smartly but some were dressed so loudly or absurdly that both Cameron and Mick diagnosed colour blindness, complete blindness and various types of psychotic disease which removed clothes sense and the ability to interpret a reflection in a mirror. A group of girls in their twenties wandered passed laughing and joking and sipping champagne. They had beautiful happy faces, lovely skin and gorgeous curves wrapped in light summer dresses. Both men's eyes followed them as they disappeared into the crowd. Mick turned to Cameron, eyes twinkling and grinning from ear to ear.

"Absolutely fantastic huh? Oh to be a new graduate today. They didn't let girls like that into the veterinary faculty back in our day did they?"

Cameron replied, "Yes they did – but only a few. Today almost 80% of new graduates are women… It was 15-20% back in the day. "

"Aye – changed days. They must have some dirty old men on the entrance committee nowadays."

"I thought you and your dad were on the entrance committee..?"

They both burst out in raucous laughter, Mick spraying beer over the arm of the sofa and coughing and spluttering while trying to punch Cameron playfully on the chin. Cameron wrestled him away and more beer was spilled in the process.

A soft undulating Scottish voice asked from the other end of the sofa, "Would either of you gentlemen like me to call security?" They both turned and beheld the face of an angel smiling at them. Deirdre Micallef stood at the far end of the sofa looking absolutely gorgeous. Her shining dark hair had flecks of grey throughout. Her hazel eyes were round and shining. Her beautiful Scottish skin, pale and ivory like, had not a line or a wrinkle to be seen. She had the rosiest red cheeks. Full red lips, moist and glistening smiled below her petite button nose. She was dressed in a clingy black dress which outlined a slim but full figure. Fine gold jewellery – ear rings, necklace and bangle finished the outfit superbly. She had black leather dress shoes with small gold highlights on but neither of the men took any notice of her feet.

Both Cameron and Mick grinned and rose to greet her. They spilled more beer as they deposited glasses on a small table in front of the sofa and then simultaneously wrapped her in a cosy group hug. They all smiled and looked at each other but would not let go of the hug.

"It's so good to see you both. Cameron I'm so happy you made it across…It's such a long journey for you… Is Alison here?" Deirdre asked.

"No she couldn't make it this trip. Next time hopefully." Cameron looked slightly awkward.

Deirdre turned her eyes towards Mick, "I hope Mandy is here to keep an eye on you… I saw you trying to break this man's jaw…" Deirdre kissed them both and they released her from the hug.

A waitress appeared and offered Deirdre champagne. She took a glass and they settled onto the sofa – Deirdre sitting between her two adoring friends.

She offered a toast and smiled, "To wonderful friends."

They clunked glasses and drank.

"How's Allen?" asked Mick. "Did he make the trip?"

Deirdre looked distant as she answered. "No…I'm afraid his travelling days may be over…He's doing well and in good spirits but every little thing nowadays is hard work. He finds it really difficult to walk more than a few metres. Communication is difficult with anyone other than close family... It takes an age to say a few words. The kids are looking after him this week. I think it could be a bit wearing for everybody..."

"I'm sure he'll be fine Deirdre. He'll enjoy having the kids around. They'll spoil him," Mick enthused.

She smiled. "Yes – and I have a whole week in Edinburgh to drink champagne and eat beautiful food and catch up with my favourite people."

Cameron and Mick smiled. They clinked glasses again and drank some more.

"Time for a wee-wee," Mick announced as he stood up and stretched. "You guys behave and I'll be back shortly. If another of these lovely wee waitresses appears – grab me a lager."

He wandered off towards the hall entrance and was soon lost in the crowd."

Deirdre turned her full attention to Cameron. Her smile was mesmerising.

"It's so good to see you Cam. You look great. How is Alison?"

Cameron tried to remain up-beat. "She's great. Working hard and keeping out of mischief. Too busy though – couldn't come because of social and riding commitments..."

Deirdre squeezed his hand. "Are you OK?"

Cameron looked into her beautiful face. Her eyes were penetrating and reached deep into his brain. What could he say?

"I'm fine. What do you mean?"

"You never could cover up your true feelings. You're not very happy are you?"

Cameron was taken by surprise by Deirdre's directness. There was a very pregnant pause before he answered.

"I'm not really sure how I am at the minute Deirdre. I'm a bit lost. I don't understand what's happening with me and Alison. She's not here. She could have been here. The more I've thought about it the last couple weeks I've realised she's not been – "here"- for a long time…"

Deirdre looked at him warmly and said nothing.

"I really don't know Deirdre. She's so wrapped up in her own social world that our paths rarely cross. She's always off to some function or other, or organising a function for one of her groups – tennis, riding …. She's quite the socialite. But I'm realising I'm actually getting pretty lonely…"

Cameron wondered if he was saying way too much, but it actually felt good to communicate the words and thoughts that had been niggling away at him for many weeks now.

"I wonder if she's seeing someone else. Then I feel really guilty for thinking this…but… Maybe I'm missing something. I'm sure menopause can't make you just ignore someone completely after years and years…"

Deirdre squeezed his hand more. "I think you need to talk to her Cam… Or you're both going to lose out…"

"Yeah… Easier said than done." Cameron stared into space thinking of the times he had been fobbed of with lame excuses whenever he had tried to talk seriously to Alison in the last 6 months.

Deirdre held his hand and watched as he relived events inside his head.

He turned slowly and managed to smile at Deidre. "Yes my gorgeous wee friend… I need to do something." She smiled and continued to search deep in his eyes. Cameron returned her gaze and wondered what was going on in the depths of Deirdre's mind.

He asked, "And how are you really getting on Deirdre. You look absolutely fantastic but I think I can read you like you read me. Life is not so good is it?"

She took a long time to answer. "No Cam... Some days it's absolute hell. I love Allen but it's torture watching him being tortured by his hellish disease. He's changed – anyone would change – but he's become demanding. He's become very good at emotional blackmail. Everything's my fault. Everything. His mood swings are terrible and although he has very poor coordination – when he gets pissed off he's becoming more and more violent. The Doctor's say he can't help it. I know it must be excruciatingly frustrating but he doesn't have to take it out on the closest ones to him. He won't go into respite. I'm tied to him by an invisible chain..."

Tears welled in her eyes. It was Cameron's turn to squeeze her hand to try and reassure.

"I had to get away Cam. This is respite for me. I think I'm going mad. I had to get away and be on my own to sort my head out. My biggest worry is that I might not be able to go back..."

Tears were running down her flushed cheeks and slowly dripping from her nose and her chin. Cameron put his arm around her and pulled her close. She buried her face in his chest. She felt tiny and vulnerable. She felt warm and feminine. She smelled beautiful. Subtle lavender. She cuddled Cameron on the sofa for several minutes without lifting her head. Delegates passed by oblivious to them. They were lost in their own emotional bubble.

Eventually she lifted her head and looked at Cameron. Her hair was messed up and her eyeliner had run. She still had tears in her eyes and had bubbles of tears and snot dribbling from her nose.

"I just love women with snotty noses," he announced.

A grin spread across her face and she fumbled in her hand bag. Cameron produced a wad of tissues from his pocket and she laughed and took them and tidied herself.

"My God," she exclaimed, "This must be the true confessions couch.

They both laughed.

"I will do absolutely anything I can do to help," Cameron said to her.

She once again looked into his face. She reached up with both her hands and pulled his face to hers. She stared into his eyes and kissed his lips. The moment lasted an eternity – Cam felt the softness of her lips, the warmth of her breath, the minty taste of her mouth. He could have stayed there in the moment for ever.

The tightness in his trousers however announced his second stiffy of the night and he fought hard to tell it to bugger off and leave him alone. He shuffled his bum cheeks uncomfortably on the sofa to try and keep his annoying friend as far away from Deirdre as possible and out of sight of any curious passers-by.

"I know you will Cam," said Deirdre softly staring into his eyes.

Cameron had to steel himself to remember what she was talking about.

"Well you guys seem to be catching up all right," announced Mick as he returned to the table and deposited two pints of lager and two glasses of champagne. He was unfazed seeing his two friends cuddling. Deirdre looked as if she had been crying her eyes out and Cameron looked like he was here in body only. He understood that all their close friends would have lots to share with each other and in some cases family news would be painful and difficult. He made a mental note to tell Cam later in the evening to carry his wallet and phone in his back pocket.

Mick announced, "I'll just go and find the missus." He turned and was gone as he quickly as he had arrived.

Deirdre and Cameron both sat and laughed. They helped themselves to the new drink supplies. They clinked glasses and watched the crowd ebb and flow in front of them.

After a couple of quiet minutes Cameron turned to Deirdre. He looked seriously at her.

"Deirdre… I have to ask you about Damien. What on earth happened…? Did you talk to him at all? Did you have any inkling what was going on?"

Deirdre's eyes filled with tears once again. She looked at Cameron and suddenly looked 10 years older. It was several moments before she spoke.

"I loved him Cam. I often thought that I should have married him. Not just in recent years when my life started to change with Allen's ill health but even in the early years, when I realised I had married a farmer who was tied to Shetland, tied to the land of his ancestors and would never leave. When I realised that I would always be "the sheep farmer's wife" and never regarded as an individual with worth of my own. We kept in touch. He was so nice and gentle – he always helped me when I was having doubts about Shetland, about Allen, about bringing up children. He told me that he would love me forever…there would always be a place in his heart for me…."

Her voice cracked and Cameron could not hear the next few words through her tears.

He placed his arm around her once more as she sat and sobbed.

After a couple of moments she looked into Cameron's face and quietly said , "He told me that if I ever left Allen he would leave Lydia and we would make a life together…Start fresh. He wanted to marry me… God knows I was tempted. I loved him from afar. I just couldn't leave Allen. I couldn't leave the kids. I dreamed about running away for years…"

Cameron sat in stunned silence. He did not expect Deirdre's revelations at all. He sat digesting the new information. He couldn't understand. Would Damien really have left his wife and life in Liverpool to be with Deirdre? How unhappy was Damien with his married life to contemplate running away with his uni sweetheart? He hadn't known or suspected any of this. It put a whole new slant on Damien's mental state before his death.

Deirdre's next words were barely more than a whisper. "He asked me to run away with him three weeks before he died. I turned him down…"

She stared into Cam's eyes. Her eyes were pleading, tortured. Was she asking for some sort of forgiveness? Or was she sharing a terrible secret for the first time – fearing blame and retribution.

Cameron felt cold and numb. The world wasn't making sense. He replayed Deirdre's words again and again. "…three weeks before he died…I turned him down…"

Cameron pulled Deirdre into a close embrace. She tucked her face into his chest as before and sobbed – her whole body shaking. No stiffy this time. Cameron was frozen. He didn't see the crowd passing by, he hardly even heard Deirdre's racking sobs. He was trying to make sense of the last few minutes… Had his friend committed suicide because Deirdre had turned him down..? Again..? Had this been the last straw as Damien's practice went pear shaped?

Eventually Cameron pulled Deirdre's head from his tear and snot stained shirt. She looked into his face. "Deirdre… Believe me Damien's death is not your fault… It sounds like you were the one thing in life that gave him hope in his last few months. He loved you. You are not to blame for him taking his own life. It is not your fault."

Cameron listened to his own words and wondered how hollow they sounded – Deirdre's rejection may well have pushed a man at his wits end over the edge…

"Deirdre…" He kissed her on the forehead and then stared intensely into her eyes. "You cannot believe his death was your fault. Nobody can make a man put a noose around his neck and jump. He did it himself – not you… He did it himself…"

Deirdre's eyes again looked tortured…and confused. Her beautiful face contorted with despair as she whispered, "Cam… He didn't hang himself… He slit his own throat from ear to ear and bled to death…"

Chapter 10

Cameron held the porcelain bowl and retched painfully. He had nothing left. Remnants of Salmon Coulibiac clung to the side of the bowl. Most of his fantastic meal from "Jonah's" had already been flushed away. It did not taste nearly as good second time around – especially when a considerable amount came out both nostrils. His throat and mouth tasted of sweet vomitus and his guts ached. He hung onto the bowl with both hands and drooled thick saliva from his lips. Tears mingled with sweat stung his eyes. Slowly his breathing settled back to reasonable rate and rhythm. He was kneeling in front of a toilet somewhere in the Edinburgh International Conference Centre.

A recurring vision appeared in his head. Damien Corrigan sat at his office desk and slowly and deliberately slid a scalpel deep into his throat and dragged it from one side to the other. Blood erupted from the gaping wound like water from a fire hose. It sprayed across the desk, the walls, the windows and the books on the shelves. Damien rose and twisted his body around and the blood fountain struck the walls on the other side of the room. The blood was bright red as it splattered off the walls but soon turned purple/black as it pooled on the floor below the dying man. His breathing sounded excruciating – he no longer breathed through his nose or mouth – he breathed through the gaping severed end of his trachea and he choked on the blood which was showering everywhere. Each breath was a rasping wet, choking wail. He stood for interminable seconds wheezing and wailing and then collapsed like a puppet whose strings had just been severed. His body and limbs twitched as if in an epileptic fit until the wailing stopped. The bleeding slowed to a black trickle and Cameron's friend's eyes stared unseeingly at the world he could no longer live in.

Each time the vision appeared Cameron retched again. The pain was hellish. The pictures in his head were worse.

Eventually Cameron became aware of someone banging on the door of the toilet cubicle.

"Cam... Cam... Are You OK in there?" Mick's O'Reilly's deep Irish voice boomed and echoed around the tiled room. "Open the door will you...?"

Cameron slowly rose and flushed the toilet. He unbolted the cubicle door and found Mick leaning into the doorway staring at him.

"Are you OK big boy?"

"I'm fine," answered Cam.

"Too much sherbet?"

"No..."

"Are you ill? You look like shit." Diplomacy was always one of Mick's greatest traits.

Cameron looked Mick straight in the eye. "I just learned that Damien didn't hang himself..."

Mick paused. He then spoke softly. "I'm really sorry Cambo... Lydia didn't particularly want the world to know the gruesome details. The papers announced he'd hung himself and she decided to leave it like that. Didn't want his friends to torture themselves about his final minutes... Sorry Cambo... Come on let's get you tidied up."

Mick led Cameron to the row of sinks across from the toilet cubicles and turned on some taps. They looked at each other in the mirror above the sinks. Mick put a hand on his friend's shoulder.

"Leave it alone tonight Cambo. Come and have a drink with the girls and the rest of the crew. We can talk about all this another time..."

Mick grabbed a handful of paper handtowels, soaked them in the sink and started wiping the front of Cameron's shirt.

Mick screwed up his face and asked, "You been eating fish? Smells like fucking fish?...Good job you hadn't been eating fucking beetroot. What did you do with the diced carrots?"

A slow smile appeared on Cameron's face. "I think they're still stuck up my nose."

"Better give your face a wash or you'll never score with any of those gorgeous new grads…"

The face Cameron saw in the mirror opposite had red bloodshot eyes, ghostly white skin, pale grey lips and traces of silver stubble flecked with salmon pink. His hair was matted with food debris and soaked from multiple toilet flushings.

"C'mon Mick – I think I'm looking kinda hot."

"Stunning…"replied Mick. "I'll just go and see if I can track down your guide dog."

Cameron Stuck his whole head under a running tap and blasted water onto his scalp for the best part of a minute. He then washed his face and scrubbed until he looked fresh and clean. Mick stood by the entrance to the room and watched as Cameron blasted hot air onto his face and head from a hand dryer fixed to the wall. Mick's deep Irish tones suggested, "This reminds me of a Madonna video way back in the eighties… You don't look much like a virgin though… …then again neither did she…"

Cameron grinned. "No - but we ARE the two hottest beings on the planet."

As they exited the toilet area and merged into the traffic in the foyer of the EICC Mick turned his head to Cameron and said, "And next time you decide to have a puke Cambo – please use the Gents…" Cameron glanced back over his shoulder, saw the "Ladies" sign and realised for the last fifteen to twenty minutes he had been he had been heaving his guts up in the ladies toilet block.

"Fuck…"

Mick and Cameron exploded into raucous laughter and wandered back into Strathblane hall.

They ambled through the sea of people towards the Noah's Ark Stand, casually looking at the huge array of exhibits on the way - digital radiography equipment, laboratory equipment, surgical equipment, ophthalmology gear, stethoscopes, bandages, dog cages, cat boxes, nail clippers…. There were Exhibition stands for every piece of veterinary equipment imaginable. You could spend millions of dollars here if you wanted. The technology was awesome and cutting edge.

As they approached the Noah's Ark stand Deirdre emerged from the throng looking very sheepish. Her make-up had been fixed and she looked like a model from the front page of "Vogue". She walked up to Cameron and took his hand. Mick evaporated into thin air.

"I'm so sorry Cam. I didn't mean to upset you like that. I'm so sorry."

"It's fine Deirdre. I'm a big boy now… It's not your fault at all."

"I'm really sorry Cam."

"I know you are Deirdre. Don't worry. I'm fine. How are you?"

She didn't answer, just wrapped her arms around him and gave him a long hug.

Logan Bloomsberry's voice boomed above the hubbub of the crowd.

"Where have you pikers been?" he shouted and launched himself through the throng presenting Cameron with a fresh pint of lager and Deirdre with a sparkling champagne flute.

"Refreshments," he announced then wrapped his arm around Deirdre's shoulders and turned back the way he'd come pulling her with him into the crowd calling, "Electra darling… Look who I've found…"

Deirdre stared back towards Cameron laughing and calling, "I'll be back shortly…"

Cameron grinned at her as she disappeared thinking that she was the most beautiful creature on earth. She was pure gold. She was off the Richter scale. As he stood supping on lager and staring at the air where

Deirdre had disappeared from a moment before, he felt a tug on his elbow and a soft Scottish voice asked, "Hey – do you remember me?"

He turned towards the voice and suddenly there was nothing else in the entire universe apart from himself and the beautiful woman in front of him. There was no crowd, no noise. Time stood still. He beheld the most beautiful woman he had ever encountered. She had beautiful long flowing blonde hair, sparkling blue eyes, gorgeous white Scottish skin with a smattering of small freckles scattered over her dainty nose and pink cheeks. Her smile melted his soul – she had full red lips with glistening white teeth. Her whole face had him hypnotised in an instant. He smiled at her but his brain wouldn't function...He couldn't talk.

"Hi Cameron. Don't you remember me?" Shona Hollingsworth laughed and looked into Cameron's face.

He was taking in the whole picture. Her curves were wonderful. She was dressed in a clinging blue dress which highlighted every inch of her voluptuous figure. The plunging neckline was ridiculously tantalising. Her boobs even today defied gravity and appeared even more impressive than in her youth. Delicate gold earrings and necklaces highlighted her perfect skin. She was short even on her blue stilettoes but Cameron understood that some of the best things come in small packages. She looked divine.

"My God Shona you look absolutely gorgeous." The words came out slowly but as they did a huge smile lit up her face. He bent tentatively towards her to offer a kiss and as he did she enveloped him in a long embrace. As she held him tightly he wrapped his arms around her and squeezed her gently against him. The warmth from her body was wonderful. Her boobs moulded against his chest and his hands could feel the movement of her chest with every breath. She kissed his neck and whispered into his ear. "I'm so glad you're here. I've been dying to see you again."

They relaxed the embrace but still held onto each other looking into each other's faces.

"It's so good to see you Cam. I've been wanting to talk to you so much over the last few months." Her eyes twinkled.

"It's just wonderful to see you Shona. I've been thinking of you lots too..."

Cameron bent and kissed her gently on the forehead.

"We've got a fair bit to catch up on," stated Cameron.

Shona nodded and continued to look into his face. "Yes there's been a lot of water under the bridge since we last met."

It was Cameron's turn to nod. They looked into each other's eyes. "Yes," he agreed, "I think the world is going crazy..."

Suddenly tartan-clad Harry Ainsley was unwrapping Cam's arms from Shona and he was pulling her away by the arm towards the Noah's Ark stall. "Shona darling – have a few VIPs here I'd like you to meet," he announced as he pulled her way. Over his shoulder he called to Cameron,

"Nice of you to come Cam - great to see you – hopefully have a drink later..."

Cameron stood rather shell shocked as the divine Shona was led away looking rather bemused by the man of the moment, the great Harry Ainsley.

Mick's Irish lilt sounded in Cameron's ear. "It's all a bit weird Cam. Bloody Harry seems to have the hots for Shona. He's been introducing her to everybody as if they were an item. What the fuck would she see in a scum-bag like that? The same scum-bag that's in bed with her ex-husband for Christ's sake... It's all too fucking stupid. I would swear she's not interested but she might be playing him along to see where it goes. I thought that after Harry's wife died that maybe he was shagging the Belinda bitch...but Randal is living with Belinda now and they're openly dating out and about. I don't know what the fuck Harry's up to. It's all fucking weird Cam..."

Cameron was trying hard to take in all the new information immediately after he'd just fallen in love like a sixteen year old. Mick added. "And you should think about keeping your wallet and phone in your back pocket or you're going to get arrested tonight."

Cameron had been too focussed on the beautiful Shona to realise that his fresh stiffy had gone on public display. He chuckled. The good news was that he could feel it subsiding already. He turned to Mick and punched him gently in the mid-riff.

"You're a bit fat Irish twat Mick…D'you know that?

Chapter 11

Over the next twenty to thirty minutes Cameron caught up with a large number of old class-mates and a few other friends who had been in the years above and below him at uni.

John Bowler had been one of the quietest guys in the year and had famously announced in final year that he could see himself in ten years being married with five kids but didn't have a clue how to go about it. He hadn't been on a date during his whole five years in Glasgow. Cameron was delighted to hear that he was married with seven children and lived happily in the south of England in a little village outside Romsey near Southampton. He had met his wife at the local church fete where he had a "pat the puppy stall" and had been married for twenty-four years now. Two boys and five daughters... Fantastic. Victor Braithewaite had married his childhood sweetheart from his home town of Kirriemuir and now lived in Edinburgh, where Victor was a partner in a renowned small animal practice which specialised in exotic pets and reptiles. Victor and the lovely Helen had one child - Gordon - who was now studying at Liverpool University Veterinary School and hoped to come back to Edinburgh and work for his father.

John Davidson looked old and frail. He had been an equine vet in the midlands of England but had been kicked in the head by a horse and had suffered a fractured skull, broken jaw and two broken cervical vertebrae. That was seventeen years ago. His recovery had been long and painful. He had been in a wheel chair for the best part of eighteen months. He had never gone back to equine work. He had tried his hand at small animal practice for a year or so but his confidence for even the smallest of jobs had gone. For over ten years now he had written health and safety policy for the British Veterinary Association. He was delighted to meet old friends but was a shadow of the loud, swaggering, beer drinking animal of uni days.

Eleanor Martin now Eleanor Watson had been a plump, heavily freckled, redhead who had come to veterinary school knowing that she was allergic to cats, dogs, horses and birds. Throughout her five years at University she was forever suffering from running eyes and a running nose and occasionally she had severe asthma attacks. Early in her practice days she had become desensitised to her allergens by treatment with allergy vaccines and now happily worked three days a week for the RSPCA in Newcastle with no work related health problems. She had married an orthopaedic surgeon and had two kids at uni studying medicine. She scrubbed up well. She was now very slim and fit looking and wore beautiful designer clothes. John Bowler and Victor Braithewaite were both showing her a lot more attention tonight than they'd given her thirty years ago.

Anita Reid was delighted to see Cameron. In their first year at Garscube Estate they had been partnered up in a couple of classes to do practical work together. They had spent long hours together - herding sheep on snow covered hills, learning how to pare horses' hooves, manually pregnancy testing cows and shovelling shit on the university farm. They both had a love for live music back in the day and had seen several bands together in Glasgow – including U2 at "Tiffany's Ballroom"- a small night club on Sauchiehall Street when they were a little known Irish punk band that had just released it's first single, and also The Rolling Stones at the old Apollo Theatre before they had become old age pensioners and knights of the realm. They were both in love with the punk era and had seen the Boomtown Rats, The Clash and Stiff Little Fingers several times. Anita was like a sister. There had never been an inkling of romance between the two. In fact, Cameron had realised fairly early on in their relationship that he was scared of her. She was not a small woman, had an orange Mohawk haircut and wore Faux Leopard Skin Wellingtons at the uni farm. She was loud and rather intimidating. Most of her boyfriends were more intimidating than her. Cameron was glad they got along well. The modern day Anita was larger than life. She was an extremely large lady, almost six foot tall and probably 50kg overweight. Tonight she was wearing a large black kaftan or possibly a small scout tent which bulged in all directions when she moved or laughed. She now taught reproductive ultrasonography at Bristol University Veterinary

School after stints at both London and Cambridge Universities. She was held in high esteem as a teacher and an academic. She had papers published in journals all over the world. The word was that she had no partner at the moment and had been shagging final year students which she just ate up and spat out one after the other. When she spied Cameron he thought an earthquake had hit.

"Cambo…" She shouted and steamrolled several delegates aside as she caught sight of her old pal. Her orange Mohawk had been replaced by a mass of blue-black shaggy permed hair which cascaded over her shoulders and her make-up looked very Goth…thick black eyeliner with purple eyeshadow and dark purple lips. Cameron could see a striking resemblance to Gene Simmonds of Kiss. They both grinned at each other and she pulled him into a bear hug. After a few moments the heat was stifling and he could not breathe – he had disappeared deep into her cleavage and into rolls of soft abdominal fat. His brain told him he was being suffocated by a marshmallow. When she released him he gulped air in like a drowning man. He'd lost his lager… He didn't want to think too hard about where that could be. Had he put it down before the hug or had it been engulfed in soft flesh?

"Great to see you Cambo. You look great. And I hear you're here on your own..?"

Cameron felt the first pangs of panic. Please don't try to ravage me his brain screamed.

"No I'm here with Logan and Electra and the rest of the crew…"

"Don't be shy big boy. Words got around that you're here without the missus."

Cameron stammered, "Alison couldn't make it this time around – busy with social commitments."

Anita laughed and the whole EICC shook.

"Relax Cambo. Only teasing. It really is good to see you. I miss you. I miss the old days. I really loved your company back when we all started out. We had some great times didn't we? They were magic times.

We were both innocent and naive. Life was just kicking off... Do you remember that night we tried to sneak into the Apollo through the back door when the bouncers were fighting with the Ned's in the street. My arse got stuck in the doorway which was only half open and you didn't know whether to push me in or pull me out... Then the bouncers came back and I told them that I'd fallen into the door when walking past and I was going to sue them for the injuries I was suffering. They opened the doors right up and let me out and asked us please not to call the cops."

She shrieked with laughter and Cameron laughed too. It had been a great adventure. ZZ top were playing and they had had no luck getting tickets which had all sold out within minutes of the dates being announced. On the night of the gig they had positioned themselves outside the back doors of the theatre with a bottle of vodka and a bottle of coke - planning to listen to the band from outside and have themselves a party. Then the Ned's arrived and started banging on the doors. The bouncers inside opened the door and hurled abuse at them. The Neds baited them from afar hurling profanities and empty beer bottles at them. Anita and Cameron realised that there might be a slim chance of running inside if the bouncers left the door unmanned. They were pissed as farts by then and full of Dutch courage. When 4 or 5 bouncers had run out the door to do battle with the Neds they left it standing half open. It was now or never. Cameron and Anita had made their move. It was all going well till Anita's arse clogged up the works. God that had been fun... a legendary night.

"Did Loges tell you we have tickets for the "Shack"? It's a nightclub on Rose Street. We're all heading over when we're finished here tonight? It's a brilliant club – very retro…. Plays eighties and nineties music all night. It should be a hoot. You've got to come. We've got about fifteen tickets... Talking Heads, Simple Minds, the Clash... even some Spandau Ballet for anyone who's feeling romantic..."

"Sounds great Anita but I'm hardly managing to stay awake at the minute... I might have to give it a miss tonight..."

"Bullshit Cambo – we'll have a ball. All the troops are going – Loges and Electra, Mick and Mandy, Pete and Clairey, Harry and Belinda... All the old troops... It'll be just like old times..."

"We'll see Anita. I'm pretty damned rooted."

"Is that Australian for knackered?"

"Yep – I'm absolutely knackered."

"I'll find Belinda or Harry – They have a nice wee supply of little pills and powders which can help you party for days on end… They're stinking rich now… They can afford these little luxuries."

Anita erupted in raucous laughter again but Cameron was back tracking trying to make sense of what he'd just heard. Did Anita just say she was going to ask Harry or Belinda for drugs? Pills or powders..? Speed or cocaine? Fuck – was this how his mates got off these days – on party drugs?

"Don't look so worried Cambo. We'll get you sorted before we head off to Rose Street."

No fucking chance thought Cameron. He couldn't believe where the conversation had gone. He decided to take it elsewhere.

"So how does this Belinda chick fit in? I've never met her before. She's been working for Harry for ages but now she's shacked up with Randal? – Is that all Kosher?"

"Belinda is an absolute star. She's stunning. She's got more balls than most of the blokes I know. She's the brains of the show. She's from Cambridge – mum and dad are both uni professors. Seemingly dad just missed out on a Nobel Prize three or four years ago – he's an astrophysicist. She went to uni at Harvard – did a double Degree in Economics and IT. She's got a brain the size of the universe. Her head is like the Tardis. She's just fucking amazing. I'm not sure how her and Harry teamed up – it was way before Rachel died – probably a couple of years before. Most folk thought that Harry was knocking her off but I can't see it. She's absolutely stunning and Harry is still Harry – a snobby English twat. Randal joined up and fell for her hook line and sinker…"

"What the fuck's wrong with Randal? He's got the most gorgeous wife on the planet, beautiful kids, he's making a fortune as everyone keeps telling me and he goes and…. Fuck I don't understand."

"You haven't met her yet…"Anita grinned.

"She can't be that good…And how old is she? Forty..? Fifty..? She just can't appear out of nowhere and be perfect…She's got to have baggage… She's been around somewhere off the radar for the last couple of decades. What's her story? Married? Divorced? Kids?"

"She's single and very attractive. She probably gives him things that Shona couldn't or wouldn't…"

Anita looked directly into Cameron's eyes. He was supposed to have received enlightenment from the words she had just said. His brain was numb. What the fuck was she talking about?

"Sorry Anita – I've no fucking idea what you're saying…"

"Cambo…"Anita moved closer, held his arm and leaned in to talk in his ear. The heat emanating from her was intense.

"Cambo… As I understand it… When you only get a shag on the first day of every month and on your birthday if you're lucky, and it's the same boring two and a half minutes of missionary position every time… You start yearning for something else… Anything else… The beautiful Belinda gave Randal what he'd never dreamed of and he fell for her like a ton of bricks."

Cameron stood with his mouth open. He needed a drink but his lager had not reappeared.

Anita continued. "I hear that she likes to tie people up… She likes to be tied up too… I hear she likes to inflict pain… she likes to take it to another level… she's a free spirit… there are no restrictions…she goes where her imagination takes her…"

"Where do you get all this shit?"

"Harry and Randal and I have been collaborating over recruitment of vets for NOAH's directly from university… You know how it goes. Tongues become loose after a long day at work when you head out for a few drinkees…"

"Fucking Hell… Are you working for them as well now?"

"No – I have my own little recruitment agency. Get paid very nicely too."

"And Randal tells you all the sordid details?"

"You know Randal. Can't keep his mouth shut when he's having a bevvy. Harry eggs him on – he seems to get very excited when he hears the steamy details."

"Fucking Hell... Fucking Hell..." Cameron was blown away by the extraordinary revelations. His brain took him back to Shona being led off to meet VIPs by a very smarmy Harry.

"So it looks like Harry has the hots for Shona... He's all over her like a rash tonight. It's all getting a bit fucking incestuous isn't it?"

Anita laughed so much her body rippled like a blancmange. When she finally got control of herself again she moved in close again and spoke softly into his ear.

"I've no idea what he's up to Cam. But then again I've no idea what she's up to. If I was her I'd be kicking him in the nuts and telling him to get back in his box. I wonder if she's playing games hoping that it'll piss Randal off. She's going to get burned if she's not careful."

"How much more badly could she get burned? She's lost her husband, has no job, no income, she's a laughing stock... You're telling me it could get worse?"

"The whole world is watching. If she goes on like this she'll lose the respect of all her friends and family. In the last twelve months everyone has been very much on her side but if she keeps playing games people might start wondering why Randal didn't jump sooner. If she teams up with Harry it'll look like she's just chasing the money or desperately trying to get close to Randal again. I think she's fucked unless she just pisses off out of the picture."

A waitress passed and both Cameron and Anita grabbed a pint of lager each. They clinked glasses and still looking straight at each other sucked the cold fluid in deeply.

After several moments silence Cameron announced, "It's all just way too fucked up."

Anita nodded, "You're not wrong buddy..."

After another long suck on her beer she added, "But it's great to see you. We're going to have a ball this week. I hope you're coming to all my lectures."

"Fuck – are we supposed to attend lectures this week as well as drink piss?"

They both laughed again and Anita gently punched him on the chin.

"You better come to my lectures. I'm a renowned world leader in reproduction I'll have you know."

"So I've heard. Do you tie people up too?"

The laughter erupted again and they both bounced off one another in hysterics. Cameron was still catching his breath when he became aware of someone standing very close behind him pushing into his comfort zone and breathing hot air down his neck. Just as he turned expecting to find Mickus or Loges being a twat, Anita's face lit up with a huge grin and she shouted, "Fantastic timing! Cambo – turn around and meet Belinda."

Chapter 12

Harry turned around slowly to find Belinda Martin standing only inches away. As the crowd milled around them she moved even closer until their faces were almost touching. She was an Amazon. Cameron was 6 feet tall – 183 cm and he looked up into her eyes. She was so close he could taste her breath. She was stunning. Large hazel eyes in a sculpted tanned face, an aquiline nose with flaring nostrils above sensuous full lips. Her lips were painted dark red and her teeth were luminous white. Her eyeliner was the blackest black with gold glittering eyeshadow. Her hair was thick, shining black and fell straight to her shoulders. She wore heavy gold earrings and multiple heavy gold chains around her neck which blended into her deeply tanned skin. Her skin was perfect – no wrinkles, no crow's feet, no bags under her eyes – smooth and shining and flawless.

Cameron was fixed by her stare – she was focusing somewhere deep within his head. He couldn't break eye contact. He wanted to look down. He wanted to examine in detail the shape of this stunning woman but he could not pull away from her eyes. He could see the smooth skin of her shoulders emerging from the delicate thin material of her red dress. He could sense the fall of the material as it plunged way lower than the level of her breasts – the neckline revealing smooth skin extending inexorably towards her navel. Her breasts thrust outwards towards him like beacons pushing the thin red material tight. He could practically feel her nipples brushing the cotton of his shirt. She pushed her waist against his pretending that the passing delegates were pushing her closer. She smiled at him. She was playing a game. She was used to being in control.

Anita enthused, "Hey Belinda – This is Cameron. He's one of the troops from back in the good old days."

Belinda's voice was soft and deep and very southern English.

"Hello Cameron… I've heard all about you from Randal and Harry. It's a pleasure to meet you at long last."

As she said these words she continued her intense eye contact and her breasts and abdomen squeezed ever so slightly more against him. The warmth from her body was tantalising. Cameron was sure her hips were moving within millimetres of his.

"It's great to meet you Belinda. I've heard lots about you too," replied Cameron.

There were a couple of long moments while the pair stared at one another intently. Then Belinda's face broke into a huge smile and she said, "Not all bad I hope..."

Cameron took his time and answered, "I think Anita said something nice earlier in the evening."

She laughed and Cameron felt her grind her pelvis against his – slowly, subtly but very deliberately. She never lost eye contact with him.

"I'm liking you very much already Cameron."

Cameron returned her stare and smiled back. The erection he was getting was confusing him. He was barring up again as this woman slid against him. She was stunning - over the top gorgeous, but looking into her eyes was like looking into a cold bottomless pit. This woman was a snake. Cameron just new she was a manipulating witch. She was cold and calculating despite her beautiful smile and her gorgeous looks. He wondered how many hundreds of men had fallen to her charms before. He wondered how on earth Randal could be shallow enough to be taken in by someone who came across to him as a cold manipulating slut.

"I hear you're a very talented woman," said Cameron.

She looked at him coyly from below long black lashes.

"I like to think I have some particular assets," she returned as she continued her slow grind in his pelvic region.

Cameron grinned.

"So where's your beloved Randal this evening? Isn't he a big part of the NAVH's machine? I thought he would be here with you and Harry touting for business."

"He's abandoned me… He's in Geneva. We're looking at forming an alliance with the Swiss Veterinary Association."

"So that you can hide all your loot in Swiss Bank Accounts?"

She laughed, "Hey I hadn't thought of that. Might be something to pursue though?"

"So why Switzerland? Why not Belgium or France?"

"Tax Laws and Superannuation Laws. As independent overseas investors we can make it very attractive to retiring veterinarians to sell their practices to our group there."

"But who's going to oversee these practices if you're here in the UK?"

"These days it can all be done via the internet. It's like I'm sitting in the practice manager's chair right in the building. I can have all the practice data right at my fingertips for every practice wherever I am in the world."

"And you run the practice remotely. No personal hands on involvement. Do you have any veterinary training? Do you know what makes a good practice and a bad practice?"

"You don't need veterinary training my dear Cameron. It's the same the world over. In any business. If you're making good profit then it's a good business."

Cameron frowned a little

"Do you know anything about veterinary ethics? Do you know anything about morals?"

"Cameron… Veterinarians the world over are no different from any other businessmen or women. They need to reap the rewards of their hard work. Profitability is THE most important factor in any business."

'Sorry – you've lost me. We all want to make a good living and retire happily but we all start out with the greater ideals of looking after animals and along with that comes the ideal of looking after our clients and staff to help towards that end."

"NAVH's is all for that. It's part of our mantra."

"No it's not."

Belinda paused.

"Now where's this coming from Cameron? You have something specific in mind?" Belinda continued to stare straight into Cameron's eyes. Her eyes were cold, black and challenging. Her smile however remained and the hip grinding moved up a gear. Cameron thought she might start shagging his leg.

"One of my best friends - Damien Corrigan – committed suicide after signing up to Noah's. He did charity work, pro-bono work and he looked after old people who couldn't afford normal prices by charging less in desperate situations. For doing these things you docked his pay and strangled the good name of his practice. As far as I'm aware you hounded him until he broke..."

She continued smiling pleasantly and he felt her hand grab the belt of his trousers and pull him even closer. Her eyes never left his.

"My dear new friend... You have to look deeper. What you see on the outside is never, ever how it is on the inside..."

Her other hand insinuated itself between them and started to trace the outline of his erection through his trousers. The crowd were tight around them. Other people were talking in very close quarters. They looked like just another couple trying to hear each other over the general din. She continued oblivious to the nearby delegates. She rubbed his groin and he thought he might explode.

She spoke quietly. He found it difficult to concentrate on her lips. Her hand was massaging his crotch harder and harder.

"Your friend Damien used to like this. I used to jerk him off in his office. Lydia knew. She didn't care. All she wanted was the money. All she wanted was for Damien to keep us happy so that the cheques would keep coming. She shagged Harry one day – she wanted to keep us happy if Damien wouldn't. I don't think Harry really enjoyed it. Just a quickie up the jacksy over Damien's desk. He might not have enjoyed it but he loved playing back the security tape to let Damien see what she'd been up to…"

She paused. She squeezed his dick tightly through his trousers.

"You see your friend Damien had a lot of issues to think about… He was going to run away with that neurotic little bitch from the Shetlands… He never had the guts… Oh and did you know that his oldest kid Jane has a drug problem… Not only did he need money for debts to drug dealers, he had to pay off her pimp. He also had very large bills to pay at the rehab unit. BUPA doesn't pay for that sort of thing you know…"

Cameron's stiffy had deflated dramatically. Belinda found herself massaging a groin with no form at all.

"Oh Cameron – I picked you for a stayer." Her smile was replaced by a pantomime frown.

"We'll have to meet up again later and try again."

She put her arms up around his neck and pulled his face to hers. She kissed him full on the lips and slid her tongue slowly from one side of his mouth to the other. As she released her grip she bit his lower lip and he pulled back sharply. The pain was sudden and surprising.

He looked at her as she grinned and turned away into the crowd. He clutched his lip and realised he was bleeding. When a few feet away she turned back and waved like a shy sweetheart who had just had her first kiss after the school dance.

"Hopefully catch up with you later tonight," she shouted above the noise.

Chapter 13

Cameron stood staring into the crowd. He was numb. His head was spinning. He wasn't pissed. He was suddenly sober. His brain was trying to comprehend the bizarre revelations he had just heard about one of his best friends. A friend who was dead by his own hand.

Damien Corrigan. Money problems. Marriage problems... He was planning to run away with Deirdre. He had some kind of sexual relationship with the beautiful yet hideous Belinda. He had known that his wife had shagged Harry...? Up the arse? What the fuck. His daughter Jane, the beautiful Jane – drugs and prostitution... No... No... It couldn't be true. What the fuck. That NAVH's bitch was absolutely fucking poisonous.

A passing waitress handed him a pint of lager. He needed it. He needed to settle down and focus. He skulled half a pint in one long swallow and waited till the cold fluid refreshed his wilting body. God he suddenly felt very tired. He was staring at the remaining half of his pint when a familiar face appeared in front of him. He recognised the face but it was very different from the one which he was trying to put on the shoulders of this middle aged woman in front of him. She was dressed in a green uniform. The uniform was neat and ironed and she wore a fob watch on her left breast pocket. Cameron's brain was not functioning. The woman looked grey and old but he knew she wasn't. She was as skinny as a scarecrow and had kind blue eyes sunken into black hollows below short page boy grey hair. He read her delegate's name badge and tears immediately welled in his eyes.

Lydia Corrigan looked at him tenderly as he wrapped her in his arms and started to sob uncontrollably. She cried too. They hung onto each other and sobbed for minutes which seemed like hours. The world passed them by. Eventually Cameron managed to stop sobbing and pulled back so that he could look at Lydia. He couldn't let her go.

"Oh Lydia... I don't know what to say... I loved him..."

Tears dribbled down her cheeks as she smiled at him.

"We all loved him Cam. Life is just not fair sometimes."

"How are you doing?" Cameron asked.

"We're fine. The kids are all good and we're getting on with our lives."

As Lydia said these words Cameron could only picture the beautiful young Jane – skinny and naked, lying on a dirty bed with a needle in her arm being shagged senseless by some big tattoo covered black guy. He felt sick.

"Are you sure?"

"Yes Cameron we're fine now."

Was she being a proud mother and not letting on about a private hell or had he been sold a pile of bullshit? Fuck. How on earth could he approach that one? Suddenly he saw Harry jamming his great big whanger up her arse. He cringed internally and fought the pictures from his mind.

"Are you OK Cam? You look a bit under the weather? Have you had too much to drink?"

He looked into her eyes. "I'm sorry Lydia. I get upset. Images of Damien keep recurring in my head. I hate it. I can't get rid of them..." He wasn't lying.

She took his hand. "They'll pass Cam. It'll take time. I suppose coming here and seeing all your old mates brings back memories of all sorts."

He looked at her and shook his head.

"Oh Lydia – I'm so sorry. Just so sorry... I couldn't get here for the funeral... I felt terrible."

"Hey Cameron. We knew you were with us in spirit. Your letter and your flowers were beautiful. The kids all understand that you're on the other side of the world... And we couldn't bury him until after the autopsy and all the other police and government rigmarole. The service was over 3 weeks after the day he actually died. A lot of people couldn't come. We were very glad of your support. I always felt far better after your phone calls. You helped us through a very hard time."

Cameron sighed. "If there is anything I can do to help at all you must let me know. Are you OK financially? Do the kids need anything? Anything at all please just let me know."

"We're all OK thanks Cam. He was insured up to the eyeballs and NAVH's have continued to pay his salary despite his passing…"

Cameron looked into Lydia's face. There was something there which he couldn't quite fathom. Her words sounded hollow. She seemed to be repeating a script which she had memorised for public consumption.

He held both her hands and said, "Lydia – lets duck out for a breath of fresh air and a fag."

She looked at him perplexed. "I don't smoke."

"Neither do I," he stated, "But it could be a good time to start."

He took her hand and led her through the crowd in the Strathblane Hall to the exit into the foyer and then out the main doors onto the pavement outside the EICC. She didn't complain at all. Once outside her eyes filled with tears again. They walked a few metres along the pavement till they found a convenient low wall to sit on and for a few minutes sat and watched the mad evening traffic fly past.

Cameron put his arm around her and kissed the top of her head. She leaned into him.

Her soft voice eventually said, "He didn't do it Cam. He didn't kill himself…."

Cameron said nothing. He was feeling numb.

"No-one would do that to themselves. No one would put a knife to their throat and then paint the walls of a room with their own blood knowing that their wife would be the first one to find them. Dave was the gentlest soul in the world. He would never have done that to me. Back in the early days of our marriage we had pledged to each other that if ever we found we were suffering from terminal illness and were suffering too much we'd help each other to end it. Dave's option was to plug himself into an intravenous drip, add pentobarbitone to the fluid bag and sit in his favourite chair and sup on his favourite single malt while he drifted off to sleep. There's no way he did this to himself. No way… He was murdered… and the grotesque nature of his death was a warning…"

The words hung in the still air despite the noise from the traffic. Cameron was speechless. He sat stunned. After a few moments Lydia continued.

"His throat was cut from right to left. He was right handed. Right handed people who attempt injury by this means cut from left to right. There were two separate cuts – both would have been fatal… Do you think that while you're watching your life's blood splattering across the room you'd have the wherewithal to think – that might not be enough… and do it again? Bullshit. Do you think that you might be somewhat incapacitated after the first cut? The pain , the blood loss, the inability to breathe… Somebody else did it Cam. This was no suicide."

Cameron was suddenly nauseous again. He tried to intervene.

"But surely there was CCTV footage in the office Lydia. Surely the police and the coroner looked at the security tapes…"

"There were no security tapes Cam. I had smashed the camera and the security computer terminal that very afternoon…"

Cameron did not want to ask why. Lydia continued.

"We were being blackmailed Cam. Damien had stopped complying with NOAH's demands. He had failed to follow their protocols and they had refused to make his salary payments. We were desperate for cash. Desperate. Harry explained to me that if I helped him out in certain ways then the money would be paid in full regularly. I agreed Cam. It was just hellish. I had no place to go. Damien was in his own personal hell and I thought I could help…"

"Harry bent me over the office desk, pulled my knickers down and raped me up the arse. It was shocking. It was excruciating, it was brutal and demeaning. It was horrendous. I thought I was going to die… When he was finished he patted my arse and bent to talk in my ear – he said – "Thanks Darling – that was lovely. I'll look forward to my next visit. There'll be a couple of grand in the bank tomorrow…" His delivery was impeccable… I vomited over the office floor… I'm not sure if it was from the pain or the implications of his words…He'd turned me into a whore… I needed 13 stitches"

Cameron pulled her closer to him and kissed her head again.

"I'm going to kill the bastard," whispered Cameron.

"You can't Cam… They'll kill Jane…"

Cameron was rocked once again. What the fuck was going on?

Lydia continued her voice steady, tears dripping down her face as she stared absently into the Edinburgh traffic, her brain in a different world.

"Jane was fantastic in her first year at uni. Good grades, good new friends, wonderful social life… In second year however the wheels started to fall off. Her grades declined, she didn't come home in the holidays, she was for ever needing money. When we did manage to see her she looked terrible. Skinny, pale, bloodshot eyes… She had horrendous mood swings and would go off at the slightest little thing. We thought it might be boyfriend trouble. We thought she might be pregnant. We were distraught. Damien was an absolute mess. Then one day she just disappeared. She wouldn't return calls. She stopped going to classes. None of her friends had seen her. We called the police. They were less than helpful…She's a grown woman – she can do whatever she wants… We hired a private detective… It took him several weeks… He found her in a brothel in London – working to pay for heroin."

Lydia sobbed and her shoulders shook. Cameron just held her. After a couple of minutes she started talking softly again.

"It was a battle but we eventually persuaded her to come home. We got her into a rehab unit just on the outskirts of Liverpool at Whiston. Not an ideal place but the nurses, social workers and psychologists there are wonderful people. It's cost us a fortune but she's now living at home and has a part-time job at one of Damien's favourite bird rescue centres where the girls are very understanding and helpful... They just adored Damien and would do anything to help. Private counselling and psychiatrists are very expensive. Worse than that we had to pay off drug dealers who'd quietly turn up in the middle of the night demanding cash. Worse still, we've paid tens of thousands to the evil pigs from the brothel who threaten to lure her back and insist she still owes them. The police although sympathetic cannot stop these people form harassing us... So, over the last couple of years cash flow has been very important to us. Selling to NOAH's gave us a lifeline but we still needed income to live and to deal with Jane's nightmare."

Cameron's voice came out in little more than a whisper, "Oh God Lydia...I'm so sorry. I had no idea. Does anyone else know?"

"I'm not sure. I'm treated like a leper these days in the industry. Very few people will talk to me about anything. But NAVH's call the shots and I live with it...I'd be pretty sure Deirdre Micallef knows a lot more than she let's on."

Cameron felt sick in the stomach again...He realised that Lydia probably knew about the relationship between her dead husband and the beautiful woman from Shetland.

She continued. "Harry... the black bastard... Decided to apply some leverage to me when Damien was not complying with NAVH's threats. He was trying to stir the pot one day with me and announced that he knew Damien was planning to leave me for Deirdre..."

"He's just the lowest bastard..." Cameron interjected quietly.

"I already knew. I had stumbled across the odd e-mail from her over the years which seemed a little too cosy, but one day back in June 2014, I was rummaging around some office files looking for some old invoices when I found a stash of letters from her. She talked about her loveless marriage and her husband's problems and how she'd wished she'd married Damien instead of him. I said nothing but kept an eye on the stash. As it grew over the months I realised that they were hatching a plan to run away together..."

Cameron sat in silence. He did not know what to say.

Lydia continued. "I wasn't broken hearted. To be honest I was extremely sad... But I knew I had a big part to play in this long distance love affair. I actually felt sorry for them both..."

Cameron was not making sense of any of this now.

She turned and looked up into Cameron's face. "Cameron....Over 10 years ago I realised that things were not quite right in our marriage. I didn't understand what. I spent a lot of time inside my head – searching for answers. When it hit me it was the greatest epiphany. I've only ever shared this secret with Damien and several very close friends..."

Cameron was wondering what on earth was coming next. Holy shit his brain was screaming – do not tell me you're an axe murderer...

"Almost ten years ago Cameron, I realised I was gay. I had to tell Damien. We were best friends. I loved him – I still love him. He was blown away. He was devastated. He still loved me – worshipped me... We decided to live with it until the kids were old enough to fend for themselves and then see where life took us. I don't blame him for his relationship with Deirdre however bizarre it may seem. I still loved him. I'm sure he still loved me."

Cameron's jaw had dropped. He sat staring unbelievingly at his lovely friend. No wonder she had aged so much. How much shit could one person deal with?

Cameron sat and stared at her. No words would come. She reached up and kissed him on the cheek. She then added, "I still love you too. It doesn't change that."

He smiled. "I really love you too."

They sat and looked into one another's faces.

Cameron looked confused for a few moments then asked, "So there's no chance of wild sex with you this week then is there?"

For the first time tonight Lydia's face broke into a grin and she started giggling.

"No Cameron – I might have to give that one a miss…"

They laughed and hugged each other and sat once again staring into the traffic.

Eventually Lydia spoke. "So when Harry realised that he had no extra leverage with this revelation about Deirdre he let it slide… It was several weeks later when he asked how Jane was going in rehab and explained that Damien was not complying with his requests. It was then that he raped me."

Cameron let the word rape run around in his head. Lydia had already admitted that she had agreed to help Harry out… but the brutality of the sex was ridiculous…"

"Damien had had enough of NAVH's dictating policy to him and using blackmail techniques to force him to comply. He decided that he had to take it to the BSAVA. He couldn't be alone. He suspected that the growing empire was built on the manipulation of many other naïve and vulnerable veterinarians. He contacted the BSAVA and outlined his worries. He was given an appointment with the BSAVA president himself. The day before his appointment at the BSAVA Harry turned up at the practice unannounced in the middle of afternoon.

Harry had way too much information. He knew Damien had an appointment with the president, he knew the nature of the complaints he was going to air. He was extremely pissed off and seemed to know the details of Damien's e-mails as if he'd actually read them. Damien and I had been suspicious for many months that because we had NAVH's software in our computers they had access to material on the computers which should have been private and confidential. Even when we were in the process of selling to NAVH's we were concerned that Harry and Randal knew too much detail about us and our practice. We were under a lot of pressure to sell when we did – we desperately needed the money. We didn't follow up on our suspicions. Afterwards Damien had pondered the possibility that by opening emails from NAHV's he had let them introduce spyware into all our computers – whether at home or in the office. They seemed to know just too much…"

"When Damien would not discuss his upcoming visit to the BSAVA Harry pulled out a memory stick and stuck it on to Damien's computer. He watched Damien stare at the screen in disbelief as the video image played of me sprawled across his desk screaming as Harry raped me."

"Harry threatened that if Damien went to the BSAVA he might have to keep coming back here for more of the same or maybe head to London to a certain brothel… where he knew Jane was likely to return if NAVH's was investigated in any way at all."

"Damien threw him out of the building screaming at him that he was a vile, blackmailing bastard and promised that he would send him to jail for a very long time. Once he'd gone Damien collapsed behind the office door. I found him there sobbing like a baby. He told me everything that had happened. I went ballistic and smashed up every surveillance camera in the building and smashed the CCTV computer with a mallet."

"Damien spent the rest of the afternoon in the office. None of the other staff in the building came near the office at all. I was given an extremely wide berth by everyone working that day. At 6 o'clock every one left. I talked to Damien in the office. He was finishing a handwritten list of notes that he was taking to the BSAVA. He told me he was going to talk to the BSAVA as to how he should approach the police about our whole experience with NAVH's. We hugged for a long time. He told me he was so sorry for what had happened to me. He told me he would love me for ever."

"When he didn't arrive home for dinner by 8 o'clock I phoned him several times and just got his answer service. I drove to the Vet Hospital. His car was still there and the light was still on in the office. When I walked in I discovered a blood bath…"

"I had a mental breakdown. I was in and out of hospital for several months. I was medicated to the eyeballs. To the outside world NAVH's was wonderful. They sorted out the funeral. Got counselling for the staff. They looked like saints. Their behaviour added to their status as the caring Veterinary Group. I'm sure their recruitment numbers are sky rocketing. Before I left hospital the first time, Harry came to visit me quietly one afternoon - just a couple of days before the funeral. I had already been told that the police had found no evidence of foul play and that the coroner had ruled death by suicide. It had been reported in the press that he had hung himself...I'm not sure why but probably better for the public not to know the horrendous truth. Harry quietly informed me that I had been suffering mental illness and that NAVH's would do their utmost to look after me in the foreseeable future. They would not however extend their duty of care to look after Jane if she decided to return to her previous bad habits and mode of earning. He felt that this was an imminent possibility if NAVH's were defamed in even the slightest way by any member of the Corrigan family. She was a very vulnerable girl and was likely to suffer mentally if any mudslinging occurred after the untimely death of her father."

"I'm sure he returned to the Vet Hospital the night Damien died. Do you remember that he's left handed? The scalpel and blade that cut Damien's throat were "Captain" brand. We didn't use them at all in the Vet Hospital back then. That's the brand of a company that's in bed with NAVH's – they insist that all their practices use them. Damien wouldn't have them in the place. He said they were cheap, poorly made and broke too easily. Scalpels and blades we sourced elsewhere – much to NAVH's disgust. You knew that Harry's wife died in a car crash a month after Damien's funeral?"

Cameron nodded slowly confused by the sudden change in direction.

"I was back in hospital for about a month immediately after the funeral. When I came home there were several messages from her on my answer machine. She was desperate to come and see me. In the messages she stated that she had some very important information for me. She needed to see me in person. When I called her back I found out that she was already dead..."

Cameron felt numb.

"I'm sure she knew the truth about Damien's death... Or at least had her suspicions."

After a long pause she continued.

"Do you remember Harry's son Eden? He was at uni at the same time as Jane. I found out recently that it was him...Eden Ainsley...that introduced Jane to heroin. He gave her her first shot...showed her how to do it... Eden fucking Ainsley... There are no coincidences in this life Cameron... All you have to do is join the dots..."

Chapter 14

Cameron and Lydia stared into the traffic. Lydia reliving the hell of the last couple of years. Cameron coming to terms with the hell he had been blissfully ignorant of. They both stared unseeingly, lost in their own thoughts. Cameron was rehashing Lydia's revelations. Damien murdered? June a rehabilitating drug addict who'd been drawn into prostitution to pay for her habit? Harry Ainsley a murderer...that could just not be true. Harry Ainsley a rapist, a blackmailer...No... Fuck off... Surely Lydia had lost the plot. Surely the police could not have got it wrong. Lydia had lost her husband and been hospitalised with a mental breakdown. Surely this was all in her imagination... But Belinda had told him that Harry had had sex with Lydia. She had told him that Harry had shown Damien the recording of him shagging Lydia. They both were telling the same story. Was Harry such a fucking arsehole? If he could go this far maybe murder was within his capabilities. Fuck... Fucking fuck. So how did Randal and Belinda fit into this mess? Were they innocent bystanders or tied up in the whole filthy mess too. Belinda had struck him as a psychotic bitch within moments of meeting her. Randal though... Cameron thought he'd lost the plot when he left Shona...But being mixed up with these two, who knew where his moral compass sat these days. Who knew what the fuck he was thinking? Fuck...

Several young vet nurses dressed in green uniforms, similar to Lydia's, appeared out of nowhere laughing and talking on the pavement in front of them.

"Lydia – we've been shouting to you for ages. You'll need to get your hearing aid checked," a small round girl with a lovely toothy grin announced to Lydia. "We've been at the door of the conference centre shouting to you for ages but you were away with the fairies. Our RANA opening night raffle is about to be drawn and you promised to present the prizes. Are you coming in or are you too busy chatting up this awesome looking bloke?" A ripple of laughter came from the other girls in the group.

A taller skinny girl with red hair and rather large buck teeth joined the cause, "Yes you'd better come now Lydia or they'll get somebody else to do it. You'll get your photo in the RANA magazine...It might even get in the Daily Record... this is your chance to become world famous."

All the girls were laughing loudly and the skinny girl took Lydia's hands and pulled her up off the wall. A small cheer rose from the bunch. Lydia looked at Cameron and smiled.

"I'd better go and become world famous now. Are you coming in to watch?"

Cameron smiled back at her. "I might just sit here for a minute or two and enjoy the Edinburgh sights."

She smiled back. "Don't sit there all night. I'll be back to check on you in a few minutes."

She let herself be led away by the group of laughing girls towards the entrance to the conference centre and Cameron watched them until they disappeared into the building. It wasn't long before he was staring into the traffic again and wracking his brain for evidence of truth in Lydia's horrendous story.

He kept coming back to Belinda Martin. She was a total unknown. Nobody knew much about her. She had appeared out of nowhere. She seemed poisonous. She had to have a history. Time for a chat with Mr Google.

He pulled his phone from his trouser pocket and hit the Google logo. He Googled "Belinda Martin". Multiple hits came up for various Belinda Martins across the globe. Facebook and Linkedin had several dozen. He refined his search – "Belinda Martin NAVH's". He hit the first entry that came up. Here she was – Belinda Martin Business Manager NAVH's...Joined company 6 years ago...particular interests – practice management, computer software and programming, accounting, public relations.... She had a double Degree in Economics and IT from Harvard

University. There were several photographs – none in glamour gear with plunging necklines – most looking business like and studious. There was no personal info at all. Cameron searched a few other Belinda Martin entries but none were related to the NAVH's business manager. He searched for several minutes but could find no history previous to her arrival at NAVH's.

Next he typed in "Harvard University Graduates". Thousands appeared but he then narrowed the search to Belinda Martin. There were no Harvard graduates called Belinda Martin. Shit. Dead-end. Maybe she's been married…? Maybe she' changed her name for other reasons Cameron thought. He typed in "Harvard Graduates Belinda". There appeared to be several hundred. Too many to go through. He needed to try a different tack.

He typed in Astrophysicists Cambridge University. A long list of names appeared but none with the surname Martin. Her father could be in there but if she'd been married his surname – her maiden name - could be anything… He took a punt and typed in "Astrophysicists Cambridge University 1980's". Three names came up. Anthon Lewis 1954-2014, Jesu Martinez 1931-1998 and Jonathan Mowbray born 1939. Let's try the live guy – Anita had talked about both of Belinda's parents in the present tense…surely that meant they were alive. He typed "Jonathan Mowbray Astrophysicist" and a huge number of results came up. He went with the Wikipedia entry. He scanned through the text and was delighted to read –

"….Nobel Prize nomination 2002… Black holes and anti-matter… worked for several years in collaboration with Stephen Hawking - British theoretical physicist and cosmologist…

Married to Evelyn Deschamps Professor of Ancient History Cambridge University…

….two children Benjamin Mowbray and Pascal Mowbray…."

"Fuck…" Cameron swore out loud, "No frigging daughter."

He was frustrated. There couldn't be too many families with professors at Cambridge uni as both parents. These guys fitted the right age group as well…"

Was this a dead end? Had he missed something or misinterpreted something?

Maybe he had some crossed wires. Either of the two boys could be married to Belinda despite her different surname. Maybe Belinda's father-in-law almost won a Nobel Prize.

Cameron returned to the Harvard Graduate list and typed in Benjamin Mowbray.

His eyes lit up wildly as he realised he'd hit the jackpot. Benjamin Mowbray graduated from Harvard University in 1998 with a double Degree in Economics and IT. Cameron read quickly through the biography and stopped in his tracks stunned when Benjamin Mowbray's graduation photo lit up his mobile screen. The face was unmistakable – the skin, the nose, the eyes... Benjamin Mowbray was Belinda Martin. No mistake. Benjamin Mowbray WAS Belinda Martin... It was definitely the same person. He enlarged the photo and stared into the face that he had stared at less than an hour ago.

His brain screamed. She's a fucking bloke. Jesus Christ. She's a fucking bloke. She's had a fucking sex change. Jesus Christ. Oh Fuck... He sat for minutes staring at the small screen. His brain was slowly digesting his discovery. What the fuck happened he wondered. A sex change?

Fucking Hell.

Fuck.

Randal is shagging a bloke....

That bloke was holding my dick... Holy Shit...

He flicked back to Google and typed in "Benjamin Mowbray". A huge number of entries appeared. He flicked through the first couple of entries – not the correct Benjamin Mowbray .He tapped on the third Benjamin Mowbray entry and almost fell of the wall he was sitting on. The entry read , "Wall Street Journal 12 August 2005 - Employee at Michigan State Bank of 6 years Benjamin Mowbray jailed for 4 years on charges of insider trading , computer hacking and internet fraud... money has not been recovered... Graduated from Harvard 1998... Loner...Unrepentant..."

Cameron stared at the screen.

He checked some more. There were no entries for Benjamin Mowbray after 2005. He checked again. None.

He then went on another hunt for Belinda Martin. As if by magic she first appeared on the planet in 2011.

Chapter 15

As Cameron walked back towards the EICC there were many things on his mind. Was Damien murdered as Lydia insisted? Was his lovely friend Lydia batting for the other team? She said so herself... He'd fancied her back in the day. What a waste. He knew Harry Ainsley was a snake but just how venomous was he? Was he capable of rape? Of Murder? Harry's wife had died in a car crash before she could give some unknown information to Lydia... Amongst all that, something else was worrying him and kept pushing everything else aside. He had had his dick fondled by a bloke...And he had been enjoying it... Come on Cam get a fucking grip... You hated every second... No I fucking didn't...I was worried at one point that I was going to explode in my undies. Jesus Christ. I am not gay. I did not know. Fucking hell.

The EICC was now lit up like a Christmas tree although the sun had not set. It was stunning to look at. He fell into an old habit and pulled out his phone again to take a "Selfie" in front of the beautiful building. He took several with different views of the EICC and the banners proclaiming "Welcome to The Word Small Animal Veterinary Conference 2017". He thought he would probably remember this conference for reasons other than improving his veterinary knowledge and skills.

His phone stated it was 21:36. He flicked to Australian time... 08:36 on Monday. He'd received no message or missed phone call from Alison. She was probably too busy. It would be peak hour traffic back home. He considered ringing but probably not a good time... Lame excuse. He pocketed his phone and wandered back into the building.

As he entered the Strathblane Hall he realised that most of the delegates had moved to the far end of the hall and were listening to speakers standing on a small stage. He wandered up to the throng and joined them to listen.

A sharply dressed middle aged man was smiling at the crowd and gesticulating. His suit looked Italian and his accent sounded the same.

"...So once again ladies and gentlemen. Thank you very much for attending the World Small Animal Veterinary Conference. All the committee members and myself hope you have a wonderful time here. We look forward to seeing you at both educational and social events. Lastly I would like to thank all our sponsors for helping us make this great event possible. Particular thanks to Mars Ltd., Hill's Pet Nutrition and Noah's Ark Veterinary Hospitals who are our major sponsors. Please make sure and visit their exhibition stands. Ladies and Gentlemen – I look forward to seeing you all here tomorrow. Have a great night."

A round of applause rippled through the crowd. The screen above the stage stated "Thank You Professor Luigi Ancelotti – President World Small Animal Veterinary Association."

Cameron was impressed. NAVH's were major sponsors... Mars and Hill's were billion dollar companies. He wondered how much Harry and Randal had shelled out to be major sponsors here. Then he wondered why on earth Randal was elsewhere when his company was going all out to impress here. Seemed odd. You'd think you'd have the whole team here...Networking, shaking the right hands, hob-nobbing with the big boys. He assumed rubbing shoulders with the big boys could only help business.

The majority of the crowd were now turning and ambling towards the exits. Cameron stood still and looked for familiar faces. He felt a tap on the back and turned to find Loges shoving a pint of lager at him.

"One for the road old chap." He announced, smiling as always.

"Thanks Loges – you're a man after my own heart."

"The rest of the troops are over towards the NAVH's stand. Follow me. We'd better catch them. They're all heading to Rose Street." He turned and led the way through the thinning crowd.

They found William, Mick and Peter laughing uproariously with each other and the girls close by talking about the gorgeous Italian

President of the WSAVA. There were a dozen other familiar faces talking together In front of the NAVH's stand. Cameron felt his bum being pinched and turned to find Jacqui Alcott smooching up to him again. She grinned. She looked half cut. Her words came out slowly with a hint of a slur.

"So are we all going dancing?"

Cameron smiled, "I think that's the plan."

He felt a soft hand tug on his arm and then felt his hand being squeezed. He turned his head to see who else was seeking his attention. Shona was being led passed by Harry who was deep in conversation with the gorgeous Luigi Ancelotti. She looked at him with wide, beautiful, pleading eyes and whispered in his ear, "You've got to rescue me..." He stared into her eyes as she was led away by Harry who was holding her hand tightly, but was engrossed in the Italian suit walking on his other side. She continued to look back over her shoulder to him for several seconds as she was quietly dragged away.

"I'm pretty sure she's taken Cambo," Jacqui announced. "Harry's been parading her around in front of all the dignitaries all night. You'd think she was his new wife."

"Yeah...,"Cameron sighed still staring after her. "All seems a bit fucking weird to me."

"Yes. I can't understand it. He becomes a worse slime ball as he gets older," Jacqui added.

Cameron turned back to face her.

"How do you mean?"

"I hear he's been knocking off quite a few of his new clients. Turns up like a knight in shining armour to buy their practices – older career girls with no business partners and little pension money stashed away. He offers them a good deal and they think he's Sir Lancelot. They become smitten and he helps himself to the icing on the cake. Once the deal is done and they think they've scored both financially and personally he usually just drops them like a hot potato and they're left in the lonely hearts club again. He's got one or two dangling on a thread at the minute. He always was a slime ball but I think he's getting a lot slimier these days..."

"So why is Shona hanging around? You'd think she wouldn't want a bar of him?" Cameron asked.

"She's lost the plot..."

"You're not wrong."

Loge's booming voice sounded over everyone's heads.

"OK folks we're off to Rose Street. We can get cabs out front. We're booked in to "The Shack". If you haven't got a ticket already I've got seven or eight here."

About half of the party started plodding towards the exit to the hall while the other half crowded around Loges needing a ticket. Cameron waved a couple of twenty quid notes towards Logan but he waved them away saying, "Harry's treat – buy him a drink when you get there." Once all the tickets changed hands it seemed that the numbers were just right. Everyone who still needed a ticket now had one. They moved en masse out of Strathblane Hall and through the foyer. Jacqui held on to Cameron's arm all the way chattering inane rubbish about how nice Edinburgh was these days and how she missed living in a civilised place... When she decided she best have a wee stop in the foyer ladies room, Cameron quietly stole away with the people in front hoping to escape her clutches. He scanned the horizon looking for Shona. She was already outside and still attached to Harry who was still trying to crawl up Mr Italy's bottom. He spotted Deirdre chatting to Peter and Claire and hoped he wouldn't be too conspicuous if he sped up and joined them. En route he was apprehended by a very drunk Victor Braithwaite accompanied by John Bowler, John Davidson and Eleanor Martin who were in a very similar state. Victor grabbed him by the arm and linked his arm through Cameron's so that he could not continue on his mission to join Deirdre and the Bloomsberrys. Victor exclaimed to his drunk pals,

"Isn't it so good to see Cameron guys? It really is wonderful to see you Cameron. It's great you could make it here."

Cameron relaxed and beamed at his old friends who were nodding in agreement and announcing, "Fantastic", "Just Brilliant", "Such a great effort to come all this way…"

Cameron addressed the group. "It is fantastic to be here but it's even better to see you all. You all look magic. Absolutely magic…. I still can't believe that you have seven kids John…"

They all laughed and John Bowler grinned from ear to ear and said, "I can't believe it myself some days but it's true…"

Cameron added, "And all you boys look pretty good but Eleanor you have absolutely bloomed. You look absolutely beautiful tonight."

All attention turned to Eleanor who turned as red as a beetroot with embarrassment.

"Thank you Cameron," she eventually replied. "You're looking rather handsome yourself this evening."

Cameron laughed. "I think you need to get your eyes tested dear."

They all continued to laugh as they walked through front doors of the EICC and out onto the pavement. There were two loaded taxis already departing from the taxi rank with windows open and cheering from the passengers. "Hurry up you slackers," "See you there…"

"Order 4 pints of Lager and a gin and tonic for Eleanor please," shouted Victor at the departing square black vehicles.

"That's an awful lot for Eleanor to drink," stated John Davidson dryly.

Cameron had missed Scottish humour and laughed out loud.

The next taxi on the rank had already driven forward and the men opened the doors and ushered Eleanor inside first and then all took seats around her.

The mood in the taxi was jovial. Everyone quietened and watched the beautiful city go past. The streets were still filled with tourists even at 10 o'clock on Sunday night. The weather was amazing. The skies were still light blue and golden sunlight spilled between the high buildings. The traffic was a lot quieter than earlier in the day but still hectic enough. The air was filled with music from eateries and pubs which were still doing great business. The trip was fascinating. The Castle appeared high on their right as they drove alongside Princes Street Gardens. It was a stunning site. The sun shone on the ancient masonry and it seemed to glow golden. Floodlights from the gardens shone onto the massive rock formation below and coloured it purple and blue. It was magnificent.

Once on to Prince's Street they could see people sitting on the grass in the park and walking amongst the gorgeous gardens. They admired Scott's Monument in the distance and watched as trams flew passed while they waited at traffic lights. As they turned left from Prince's Street onto Frederick Street they passed a road traffic accident on the other side of the road. A small silver Mercedes convertible had smashed into a lamppost. It's bonnet had been smashed and had buckled badly. Yellow flames were licking around the sides of the bonnet. The windscreen was smashed and buckled too. Luckily both doors were open and the driver and passenger had been pulled from the wreck and were receiving assistance on the pavement away from the vehicle. Sirens were wailing close by and as they passed two police cars screeched to a halt blocking traffic across the three lanes travelling back towards Prince's Street.

Everyone in the taxi stared back at the unfolding drama.

"God I hope they're all right," Eleanor said quietly.

"Looks like they're luckier than poor Harry's Missus…" stated John Davidson almost in a whisper.

Cameron looked across the interior of the taxi at him. He'd heard that she'd died in a car accident but his interest in the details had now been heightened. "How's that John?"

"Don't you know the story Cam?"

"I only know she was killed in a car accident," he replied.

"Yes. Poor woman. Rachel… Lovely Rachel… had a head on with a tree less than a hundred metres from their country house in the Cotswolds. Harry had just arrived home late in the evening from a business trip and was pulling into the drive just as Rachel's car came hurtling from the direction of the house. It sped passed him and skidded out onto the main road. She was travelling at a ridiculous speed and Harry jumped out of his car and ran after her waving and shouting. He stood in the middle of the main road watching her rear lights fishtail up the road with the noise of the engine screaming like a banshee. At the first corner she was travelling way too fast and the car flew off the road straight into a tree."

"Harry said that the crash sound was sickening. He sprinted up the road and reached the car in less than 20 seconds. He tried to get her out of the car but the doors were jammed shut. She wasn't moving – she was slumped in the driver's seat. He could smell petrol. He just couldn't get her out. The vehicle was suddenly on fire and he had to pull back because of the flames. Then there was a huge explosion which blew him back onto the road. Rachel was incinerated. She didn't stand a chance. The police found Harry crawling on the road. He had serious burns to his hands and needed a head wound he acquired during the explosion stitched up. The coroner said that she was alive with few significant injuries other than a broken ankle immediately after the crash. She was likely to have been concussed and unconscious. She died in the fire. Traces of amphetamines and cocaine were found at autopsy. She had been suffering from major depression for years according to Harry. The drugs were a recent problem – an attempt to escape the depression. It almost killed him. Poor Harry… And now he lives knowing she was alive in the wreck of the car and he couldn't get her out. He watched while she died."

The whole taxi was silent. All lost in their memories of the lovely Rachel.

Cameron was lost in thought too. Rachel had died wanting to talk to Lydia – she had something important to tell her. Was she wanting to tell her about Harry's involvement in Damien's death? Was she wanting to tell her of some other secret she'd discovered about Harry or NAVH's? Harry couldn't rescue her… How hard did he try? Did he try? Couldn't he have pulled her through the smashed windscreen? Was it convenient that she died? Maybe he knew she was going to talk to Lydia... He seemed to know everything else... Was it a fluke that Harry arrived just at the right moment to see her car leave the house? Did she know he was coming home?

It was interesting that they found both cocaine and amphetamines in her system...both the drugs he'd been assured Harry could supply him with tonight. If she was off her face on drugs how the hell could she have driven the car anyway? Maybe she was unconscious before the car hit the tree. Maybe she was unconscious before she got in the car...Maybe someone else had driven the car and had gotten out after the smash. Maybe Harry's head wound was from hitting the windscreen. He could have climbed out and left her in the vehicle...Pulled her into the driver's seat when he climbed out. Cameron's mind was racing. Inside his head he could see Harry climbing out of the car. He saw him reaching under the bonnet and cutting the fuel line. As Harry lit the match Cameron forced himself back to reality. Wake up to yourself you arsehole. You're away with the fairies. You're letting your imagination run riot. Then sickeningly he saw Harry jamming his whanger up Lydia's rear end... He could hear Lydia's voice again. "There's no such thing as coincidence... Just join the dots..."

The dots painted a disturbing picture - but Harry, once again, came out smelling of roses...Poor Harry.

Chapter 16

The taxi emptied its load onto the pavement outside the "Shack" nightclub in Rose Street. The foot traffic on the pavement was still busy. Pubs and clubs along the street were making the most of the beautiful summer's evening. The smells of delicious food, the clinking of glasses and the banter of late night revellers filled the air.

The outside of the "Shack" was illuminated by small floodlights. Banners and posters advertised "Comedy Nights", "Golden Oldies Nights" and live acts that would play there in weeks to come including "Depeche Mode", "Alison Moyet" and "The Buzzcocks". Cameron was impressed. These were bands from his youth. No huge superstars but solid bands which had affected the music and the fashions of the times. The "Buzzcocks" had been the very first band he had ever seen. They were the support band to "Joy Division" at the Caird Hall in Dundee when he was still in High School. The Buzzcocks were a small almost "Punk" pop band and had wound the crowd up very nicely. When "Joy Division" hit the stage with manic lead singer Ian Curtis dancing as if in an epileptiform fit and his deep booming voice letting Dundee know how miserable he was, the place went crazy. It was Cameron's first introduction to mass hysteria and he loved it.

He was staring at the posters and dreaming about bygone days when another taxi pulled up behind him. Mick, Mandy, Peter, Claire and Jacqui poured out onto the pavement. They were in fine form. Peter was loudly berating Mick for some previous misdemeanour and the girls were practically crying with laughter and having problems walking because they could hardly breathe for laughing. Peter was paying the cab driver while aiming a barrage of profanities at Mick.

"You're just a fucking Irish Dickhead...You cannot do that you arse...And if you use fucking language like that again in front of my wife I'll remove your testicles…And I can do that you know…I'm a vet…I do it for a living…"

The girls were holding onto one another for fear of falling over and Mick was nonchalantly standing on the pavement scratching his arse.

Cameron turned and smiled. He missed this absurd behaviour.

Victor Braithwaite shouted from the door of the club, "Come on you lot – we're losing precious drinking time."

Knowing glances flashed between Cameron, Mick and Peter. The all looked bemused. Back in the uni days Victor had been a two pot screamer… Once he was on his second drink he was usually completely off his face drunk. They knew that Victor was likely to either lose consciousness soon or become extremely ill. Cameron thought that his duel with John Bowler for the affections of the lovely Eleanor may have been what was keeping him upright at the moment… The evening could get rather interesting…

Everyone moved towards the entrance to the club and Cameron linked in with both Jacqui and Claire and escorted them to the door. Tickets were shown to the doorman and they were all ushered into the foyer. The foyer was a fairly small room with walls plastered over and over with posters of upcoming gigs and previous nights of revelry. The noise was deafening. Music was pounding through the walls. A second doorman positioned at a large double inner door shouted, "If you can just hang on a moment, Phoebe your hostess for the evening will take you to your table."

Cameron and his friends all grinned at one another.

Mick shouted back "Are we going on an airplane?"

Very soon Phoebe appeared through the double doors. She was dressed in a school uniform two sizes too small with boobs trying to fight their way out of her blouse which was unbuttoned almost to her naval and a very short pleated skirt revealing her red knickers and stockings and suspender belt. She had jet black hair braided into two pigtails and a face made up like a pantomime dame. "Classy joint'" thought Cameron. School obviously hadn't been too kind to her as she looked more like a worn thirty six year old rather than an effervescent, fresh sixteen year old.

"Hello. My name's Phoebe," she shouted. "Please follow me and I'll take you to Mr Ainsley's table. We'll be serving finger food in about twenty minutes time. All your drinks are taken care of by Mr Ainsley – please just ask myself or any of the other waitresses in the club when you require drinks and we'll bring them to your table. If you're all ready we can head on in. I hope you enjoy your evening."

The bouncer opened both doors wide and the small party walked into a different world. The music was deafening and pumping. The lights were crazy. Flashes of red, green and blue light pulsed with the bass beat of the music, laser lights lit up the misty air above a mass of dancing bodies and every few second lights blasted up through the mist on the floor. The spectacle was impressive.

As Frankie Goes to Hollywood hammered out "When Two Tribes Go to War..." Phoebe led them through the crowd at the edge of the dancefloor towards the stage where a DJ dressed as a nun was gyrating and waving to the crowd. The crowd in front of the stage was sea of sweat soaked souls moving as one and waving back to the DJ. He had them in the palm of his sweaty hand.

About five or six metres from the stage Phoebe turned abruptly left through more dance watchers and climbed up four or five steps into an alcove. Within the alcove were two long tables and lots of comfortable chairs and sofas. Harry rose from a sofa where he was sitting with Luigi the supermodel and stepped forward to welcome the new arrivals. The whole alcove looked out over the entire room and was separated from the general public by a small wall covered in plastic plants. Surprisingly inside the alcove the noise was far less than outside. Phoebe turned and talked loudly rather than shouted.

"Make yourselves at home. There's champagne in the buckets on the table, glasses there too. I'll take orders for beer and spirits now and I'll be back with you shortly."

As she finished her announcement Harry beamed at them all with widely outstretched arms.

"Welcome everyone, welcome… Let's have some fun."

Cameron could see Belinda standing brooding at the far end of the alcove staring out into the amazing light show. There was no sign of Shona. Had she escaped? Was she dancing? He followed Belinda's gaze out into the sea of humanity which was bouncing up and down rhythmically in front of the DJ's stage. As his eyes got used to the pulsing lights he spotted Loges and Electra deep in the Mosh in front of the DJ. As he watched he spied two smaller beings dancing alongside them – one dark haired and one blonde haired… Shona and Deirdre… Fantastic…

His train of thought was interrupted by Peter handing him a champagne flute.

"Cheers big boy," Peter said clinking his glass with Cameron's. "Let's skull this quick and then show these Edinburgians how to really dance…"

Cameron grinned at his old mate. He knew Peter was about to put on a show.

Everyone in the alcove downed their drinks.

Harry taking the lead as suited the occasion departed the alcove and descended the small flight of steps to join the masses. He was already in the groove and gyrating his hips and waving his arms like a man possessed. Everyone else followed and filed through the crowd at the edge of the dance floor and into the Mosh. The noise was fantastic and deafening. The bass vibrated through the floor and the air and the surrounding dancers. Everyone in the venue was in party mode. The floor felt like it was bouncing up and down as "Frankie Goes to Hollywood" screamed "Relax – don't do it…" The NAVH's party congregated in the centre of the mosh pit in front of the DJ and sang along with every word. Cameron was elated. This was fantastic. He glanced around at all his buddies. They were having a riot.

William P O'Shaunessy and John Davidson had ventured into the mass of uninhibited dancers and were giving it everything. Cameron loved it. It was so good to see his friends going nuts. He did make a mental note to keep close to both of them in case they disappeared under the waves of enthusiastic head bangers. He was worried that if he himself fell he could be swallowed by the mob and never surface again. Victor and John B were bouncing up and down and screaming on either side of Eleanor who was grinning from ear to ear and bouncing with the best of them. Mick was now sitting high on Peter's shoulders conducting the masses in song while their wives danced, bounced and screamed to the DJ. Loges and Electra were giving it everything – they had linked arms with Deirdre and Shona and were bouncing up and down as one. They were lathered in sweat – they look like they'd just been pulled out of a swimming pool. Harry was sandwiched between Belinda and Anita who were rubbing themselves all over him while Luigi coolly strutted around all three screaming the words of the song to the heavens. God this was a good gig.

Frankie faded and the intro to "Don't Leave Me This Way" by The Communards vibrated around the huge room. The crowd roared and serious dancing erupted. The NAVH's Mob formed a small circle and Harry jumped into the centre and started dancing for Olympic Gold. He didn't have the best moves but he was trier. When he stripped off his tartan jacket and threw it off into the crowd the whole veterinary contingent roared in appreciation. He then threw his cummerbund after his jacket and started unbuttoning his shirt. He stopped after revealing his naval and laughed until he could dance no longer. Mick pushed Harry back to the edge of the circle and took centre stage and performed a combination of Irish jigs and Riverdance moves while everyone laughed and clapped. Next came Peter for the performance of the night... He performed all his old tricks from the clubbing days in Glasgow... He did the splits, several backflips and performed for the whole world... He was fantastic. At the end of his solo however Cameron noticed Claire leading him quietly off the dancefloor and back into the alcove where she fanned him with a large placemat while he poured iced water over himself. Cameron wondered how far it was to the nearest hospital. Maybe they had a resus team at the club – ready for OAPs collapsing. Might have to keep an eye on Pete too.

Anita was next in as dance leader. Cameron thought the floor was bending. She was remarkably mobile and every single bit of her moved with the music. She grinned at everyone and played the sultry sex goddess wobbling her boobs in everyone's faces and forever touching her hand to her gigantic bum and blowing on her finger to indicate just how steaming hot she was. She eventually pulled Belinda into the centre of the ring with her and they performed as if they were shagging each other in every which way they could…Backwards…forwards…There was much boob fondling by both and Cameron wondered exactly what he was watching… He still couldn't decide which gender he was bracketing Belinda in. He/She was making a good attempt to look very bisexual/lesbian/omnisexual….whatever.

The Communards segwayed to the "Stranglers" and serious bouncing and pogoing took over as they let rip with "No More Heroes." Victor, John and Eleanor grabbed Cameron and linked everyone together and they bounced themselves silly for the duration of the song. They were soaking with sweat when the music slowed and Midge Ure took up the lead with the community singing. "Ultravox" and Vienna. An all-time classic. Cameron new every word. The circle had reformed and Shona was in the centre duetting with Midge and moving like a goddess. My god she was so feminine. She approached Cameron and pulled him into the centre of the circle with her where he performed like an opera star. They sang the whole song. Cameron's performance was way better than Midge's. He posed melodramatically with every emotional intonation of the song. As the song ended he took Shona in his arms and held her as she collapsed towards the floor in an astounding Torville and Dean moment. The NAVH's bunch shouted and applauded the performance – probably one of the best ever seen in the "Shack".

Cameron continued to hold Shona with his arm around her waist as they took up positions on the edge of the circle. Loges and Electra were next to perform. They stood together in the centre the group and waited for their music while the DJ announced up and coming events and "Specials" at the bar this evening. The crowd listened with anticipation for the next blast from the past. The whole room erupted as the intro to "YMCA' by the "Village People" blasted from the speakers. Loges and Electra were in their element. They led the whole crowd – never mind the NAVH's bunch - with the actions for the iconic song. It was what they were born to do. Cameron and Shona danced close together throughout, happily bouncing into one another as the crowd ebbed and flowed. When the song faded she took his hand and gestured that they should go for a drink. He was happily led from the dance floor.

They climbed into the alcove and found Peter and Claire lying back in one of the sofas. Peter had a pint glass of ice and water in each hand. He was looking pale. Claire was wiping his brow with her hand and talking quietly to him. Cameron and Shona sat on the next sofa along and looked enquiringly at the Glaswegian and his lovely wife.

"Still alive then?" enquired Cameron.

Claire answered, "This happens a lot these days. Stupid bugger is sitting on the edge of diabetes and his father died of heart disease at fifty-five and he still won't look after himself properly..."

"Probably something he ate," Cameron offered.

Claire scowled back at him and Peter replied, "Aye you're probably right Cambo. Listen to the man Clairey – he's medically trained."

Shona chimed in with her tuppence worth. "Listen to your wife Pete. You should go and see a doctor in the morning and get yourself looked at. You really don't look very well at all."

As they all looked at Peter for a response the alcove started filling up with returning dancers. They were all sweat lathered and looking for refreshment. Cameron started filling champagne flutes and Phoebe appeared and started taking orders for the bar. Glasses clinked and champagne disappeared and there was laughter and merriment among the whole crew. Most of the troops stayed standing and gently swaying and foot tapping with the constant heavy background base beat. Victor had his arm around Eleanor and they were both giggling absurdly whenever Victor opened his mouth. Poor John B was staring back onto the dance floor looking rather dejected. "You've probably won out in the long-run John," thought Cam. Harry and Luigi were as thick as thieves and talked animatedly at the end of the alcove while Belinda sat on her own hitting buttons on her mobile phone. Logan and Mick were teasing Deirdre and she was laughing and pretending to punch the pair of them. The rest of the troops were busy fixing up dresses and checking lippy and singing along with every new song.

Large platters of sandwiches and canapes arrived carried by more over developed school girls. Phoebe and a twin sister appeared carrying trays of drinks and suddenly the tables were full of stunning looking food and lots of lovely alcohol. Everyone dived in. The food was delicious – sushi, small steak sandwiches, baked chicken legs and wings, fruit and beautiful cheeses – magnificent.

Cameron filled a plate for Shona and then tucked in himself. He suddenly remembered he could do with a feed – having lost his lovely seafood meal down the toilet a couple of hours ago. The food was delicious. Washed down with ice cold lager – this was the best feed he'd had since Australia.

He was very conscious of Shona next to him. Their thighs were touching and she leaned into him as she ate and laughed and joked with the others. He could feel the warmth of her body against his, could smell her perfume and could watch her closely as she laughed and talked. She was exquisite. Her skin was blemish free and so smooth. He studied every freckle. He watched as her eyes lit up and twinkled whenever she was involved in the chat. The sound of her voice was delicious. She turned to him a couple of times and caught him staring at her. She beamed and squeezed his thigh with her hand. She leaned into his ear and whispered, "You're gorgeous...But I've got to do a pee..." They both laughed as she rose and picked her way through the crowd to the exit from the alcove. She glanced back and smiled the most electric smile before she disappeared into the human sea around the dance floor.

Harry was doing a round of the tables now shaking hands and talking quietly to every individual. He was working hard. When he arrived at Cameron he slid into the seat that Shona had vacated and leaned back and stretched. He turned his head to look at Cameron.

"It's great you're here Cambo. How're you holding up? I heard your plane was delayed and you've had a rather long couple of days?"

"I think I'm beyond knackered now Harry – travelling on auto-pilot. I think when I stop I'll probably be out for the count for 24 hours."

"Just remember Cam – I've got a few little treats in my pocket that can help you stay awake and partying for days at a time. Just give me the nod if you need anything."

Cameron smiled, "I think I'll be fine Harry...Thanks for the offer...and thank you very much for the night out. It's been an absolute hoot. Later in the week we should maybe get together for a quiet pint and chew the fat. My shout. Away from the rest of the crowd..."

Harry looked deep into Cameron's eyes and held his gaze for what seemed like hours but in reality was only four to five seconds. His face was emotionless. Eventually he said, "I think that would be great Cam. There's been a lot of water under the bridge since we last saw each other. The world has changed a lot. Maybe Thursday or Friday evening if you're still going to be here?"

"Sounds good Harry."

Harry slapped Cam on the shoulder and pushed himself to a standing position.

"Better go and ply Luigi with more beer...The things you have to do to get on in business..." Harry paused after he said this and half turned to look at Cameron with the same expressionless face. "Maybe we should get you on board Cam..? There's lots of big money to be made out there. Lots...I'm not really the bad bastard that everyone thinks I am..."

Cameron returned Harry's steady stare. "I'm not interested Harry. I couldn't do it. I couldn't live with myself..."

Harry nodded and actually looked saddened by the words he'd just heard. They both continued to stare coolly at one another. Eventually Harry nodded slowly again and then turned away. Cameron thought that for a moment Harry had let his mask slip.

Chapter 17

Cameron sat and stared absently into the mass of gyrating bodies on the dance floor. He didn't hear the music. He didn't see the individuals in the crowd he just saw the liquid moving mass under the laser lights. An uncontrollable thing made up of hundreds of individuals moving as one.

He thought of the young kids who had turned up at uni back in the day. Innocent, naïve and impatient for life to begin. They were full of drive and restless and vital. The world was out there for them to come and get, and they were going to take it by storm. They all had promise – the promise of supreme confidence. The world was theirs for the taking.

What had happened? They were now tired and jaded. Changed for ever – and it seemed none for the better. Cynicism, hatred, loathing and hurt had replaced the innocence. Had manipulation, blackmail, rape and murder played a role?

He became aware that his friends in the alcove were shouting at him and waving at the dancefloor. He looked into the centre of the circle which had formed in the Mosh. The unmistakable shape of Anita was Jumping up and down and waving frantically towards the alcove.

He realised that the DJ was talking to the masses, "Where are you Cameron? Come on down…This one is for you and Anita…She says it's to commemorate the best night she ever had without sex…Thirty years ago…Come on Cameron she needs you."

Peter and Claire were pulling him up onto his feet and as he rose people in the crowd were turning and shouting to him. The roar built and built as he descended the steps from the alcove and was swallowed by the crowd. As he made his way through the wet bodies people were slapping him on the back and roaring there approval that he was on his way. When he reached the edge of the NAHV's circle deep in the Mosh, Mick and Loges dived on him and pummelled him around for several seconds then launched him into the centre of the circle where Anita wrapped him in her arms and gave him a huge wet kiss. As she released him ZZ Top let rip with "Sharp Dressed Man" and the whole dance hall went berserk. The noise was deafening and fantastic. The explosions of light were mind bending and surreal. Anita and Cameron danced like complete fools. ZZ top themselves would have been impressed with the singing and the air guitar playing. They took turns at performing ridiculous guitar solos and towards the end of the song they leaned back to back and performed the greatest air guitar duet the world had ever seen. It was a classic moment in time. The noise was deafening as the song came to an end and Anita and Cam hung on to one another and roared with laughter.

"You are the Queen of the Universe Anita," screamed Cameron above the din. "You always have been and always will be..." He hugged her tight and thought he would ignite in the heat she was emitting. She laughed and laughed and couldn't say a word.

AC/DC were now blasting the roof off with "Highway to Hell" and the crowd had swallowed Cameron and Anita whole. Mick and Loges were jumping up and down doing Angus Young and Bon Scott proud and the girls were head banging like zombies. This was so much fun. Anita thought she might die and departed for fluid therapy leaving Cameron head banging in the throng. He was caught up in the music...He was back in Glasgow in 1985...The Apollo Theatre...Bon Scott was no more...There was this new Geordie guy singing...Shit he was good...AC/DC were going to rock forever... Bon had become a Rock God...Angus Young was a freak...

Cameron was fixed to the spot head banging on the dance floor eyes closed, singing every single word and playing every single chord. He was lost in time. This was magic.

The roar from the crowd signalled the end of the song and he opened his eyes to find Shona grinning at him and head banging directly in front of him. He inched forward and put his arms around her waist and hugged her. She melted against his body and put her arms around his neck and kissed him on the lips. My god this was great. They just stood and looked into each other's eyes – both grinning like Cheshire cats. AC/DC had scored the next spot and were letting rip with "A Whole Lotta Rosie". The rest of the Mosh were continuing their riotous behaviour and bouncing around like nutcases but Cameron and Shona stood still, held each other tightly and just stared at each other. They swayed from side to side as they were buffeted by the masses but did not budge from their spot during the whole song. Cameron was hypnotised. It seemed that Shona had no urge to move anywhere else at all. As Bon Scott repeatedly screamed, "…she's a whole lotta woman…" Cameron completely agreed.

Next up was Simple Minds and "Promised you a miracle". As the intro played Cameron leaned into Shona's ear and said, "You're absolutely gorgeous…But I've got to do a pee." She laughed loudly and Cameron just loved the sound. She kissed him on the lips again and then turned and join the other girls already getting into the groove.

It was a long trek to the Gents but Cameron's feet didn't touch the ground. He was elated. The most beautiful chick in the universe seemed to be all over him. This was just too good. He loved Edinburgh…He loved beer…He loved AC/DC… He would absolutely love to love Shona…

The toilets were empty as he walked in. The drain in the urinal was clogged up with paper towels and water was over flowing onto the floor so he wandered into a cubicle. He sighed happily as he drained his bladder of several pints of Lager and a bottle or two of champagne. It was the longest pee he could remember. How on earth had he managed to hold on to all that? The relief was fantastic. He felt like a new man. He flushed and turned to wash his hands at the row of sinks opposite the cubicles. Two men had arrived and were both bent over the sinks. As he approached he realised that they were snorting cocaine. Both men were engrossed in their activity and took no notice of him as he soaped up his hands and washed in the neighbouring sink. Cameron recognised Harry's tartan pants and the Italian suit pants of Luigi Ancelotti. He looked at their faces in the large mirror above the sinks. They were unaware he was there. They were focussed on the thin white trail of powder in front of them. Cameron watched as they inhaled and then stood up straight and waited for the rush. They both looked at Cameron's reflection in the mirror. Cameron looked back at Luigi's face which had delicate flakes of white on his upper lip and around his nostrils. Luigi froze like a rabbit caught in the headlights. Harry stared at Cameron. His face once again emotionless.

Cameron said quietly, "The things you have to do to get on in business…"

Harry smiled. The smile was caustic. Harry's eyes looked dead and vacant.

Cameron slapped Harry on the shoulder and walked back into the bedlam of the dance club.

He needed another beer. He walked through the crowd of dance watchers and back to the alcove. The alcove was deserted except for one person. Belinda was slumped in a comfortable chair staring at her phone with a champagne flute in her hand. She had her bare feet resting on one of the low tables. Cameron ignored her and helped himself to a pint of lager which was sitting on a tray on another table. He turned and stared out into the club and started getting back into the music. Dexy's Midnight Runners were pumping out "Come on Irene" and the community singing was in full swing.

Belinda appeared on his shoulder and he felt her hand brush across his arse. He flinched.

She followed his gaze into the crowd. Her voice was quiet when it came.

"I'd stay away from the little blonde bitch if I were you… I hear she's' frigid anyway… For some reason she's Harry's favourite toy at the minute…" She paused. Cameron said nothing – just continued to stare into the crowd.

"Do yourself a favour Cameron… Leave her alone. You don't want to piss Harry off… You won't like Harry when he's pissed off."

Cameron turned to face Belinda. His voice was soft and controlled.

"Belinda…You remind me of someone I knew a long time ago… Both his parents were professors at Cambridge University… Just like you…

His father was nominated for a Nobel Prize – Just like you...He got a double Degree at Harvard University in Economics and IT... Just like you... Then he went to jail for fraud, insider trading and computer hacking..."

Cameron paused and stared straight at Belinda. She had turned white.

"Don't fucking threaten me Benjamin..." He paused to let the name sink in. "I might just have to have a wee word in Luigi's ear and tell him that the Business Manager of the company that are wooing him for favours at the moment has been to jail for fraud , insider trading and computer hacking... Now I've got a feeling that might piss Harry off something rotten."

He paused then quietly added, "Don't fucking threaten me."

Belinda looked shaken, pale and suddenly very haggard.

Cameron leaned in close and talked quietly in her ear.

"You'd better go and fix your make-up... Your 5 o'clock shadow is showing..."

He turned and nonchalantly walked away picking up another pint of lager as he went. He walked down the steps from the alcove and was swallowed by the crowd.

Chapter 18

Back in the Mosh Cameron bounced around until he found Loges and Electra. The rest of the NAVH's mob were lost in the music around them and dancing franticly. Fay Fife of the Rezillos was hammering out "Top of the Pops". Cameron had wanted to marry Fay back in the day. She was a punk goddess. She had been the Queen of his world. Or maybe one of the queens... He wondered what she looked like these days, wondered if she dressed in the same luminous plastic dresses, wore the same ridiculous oversized earrings and the same garish make-up. He hoped so.

Electra put an arm around him and shouted in his ear, "Isn't this just fantastic?"

"Absolutely brilliant," he roared back. "I think we should come here every night this week."

Electra laughed, "I think it would kill me..."

As if by magic Cameron found Shona hanging off his arm and he turned and grinned at her. Electra kissed his cheek and melted into the crowd.

Shona took his hand and led him through the crowd away from the DJ's stage to the back of the dance floor where the dancers were less exuberant and far less tightly packed. She put her arms around his neck and pulled him close. His arms slid around her waist again and he held her gently. She was staring into his eyes. He thought he was melting. My god she was just beautiful. Wreckless Eric sang the first words of "Wide World" and once again she kissed him on the lips. She tasted wonderful – minty, fruity, lavender...delicious. She gently chewed on his lower lip and the next time her lips opened she licked his lips and slid a soft enquiring tongue into his mouth. The sensations were wonderful. He replied in kind and they swayed quietly on the dance floor snogging like teenagers.

He could feel the warmth of her skin below her dress. His hands wandered slowly up and down her back and fleetingly touched the tops of her buttocks. Her response was to squash even closer to him. He could feel her breasts pushing into his chest, her stomach tight against his.

Wreckless Eric sang, "…I'd go the whole wide world, I'd go the whole wide world just to find her…" Cameron had never heard anything more appropriate.

Suddenly Cameron became aware that the animal which lived in his underpants was desperately trying to break out. His erection was huge and in a moment of panic he tried to manoeuvre his pelvis gently away from Shona. She stopped kissing him and looked into his face and grinned. He grinned back. She moved her hips so that they were directly in line with his and gently squashed into him as close as she could. Cameron thought he'd died and gone to heaven. His friend below was engulfed in softness of her stomach. Suddenly he had to concentrate hard not to erupt like a volcano. She was kissing him passionately again. This was the most wonderful torture he had ever encountered. His hands drifted down onto her buttocks and he pulled her in as tight as he could. My god this was wonderful. She gently gyrated against him. Oh my god this was bliss.

The dancers around them started buffeting them as the mood of the music changed and the Clash broke into "Should I stay or should I go". Shona laughed and looked into Cameron's eyes. She whispered, "I think Joe Strummer's giving us a message…"

Cameron laughed out loud and sang, "If I stay there will be trouble… If I go there will be double… So come on and let me know… Should I stay or should I go..?"

He looked into her smiling face. "Time to go I think."

Shona grinned and nodded. "I've just got to go and get my bag… I'll meet you in the foyer." She reached up and planted a wet lingering kiss on his lips and then disappeared in the direction of the NAVH's alcove.

No need to say goodbye to all his friends Cameron thought. Better to exit quietly. He wandered through the bouncing punters at the back of the dance floor and slowly wandered to the large double doors which they had all entered through earlier. He leaned against the wall and scanned the crowd. It must have been two or three o'clock in the morning and the place was still packed...and still going off...What a fantastic venue.

He watched for a few moments and then saw Shona's blonde hair bouncing towards him through the traffic at the edge of the dance floor. There was someone following closely behind. Tall, long dark hair... As Shona emerged from the throng smiling happily he could see Belinda stopping and staring from inside the edge of the crowd. She was watching Shona and her gaze met his as Shona emerged from the crowd. Her face was cold and evil. Her eyes were black and empty.

As the bouncer opened one side of the double doors to allow them to exit Cameron looked back directly at Belinda and raised the middle finger of his right hand and gently scratched the end of his nose. As the door closed behind them Cameron could still feel Belinda's eyes burning into the back of his head.

Shona linked arms with Cameron in the foyer and they walked out on to the pavement grinning absurdly.

They both scanned the street. There was very little traffic and certainly no taxis to be seen.

"Let's wander down to Frederick Street and then onto Prince's Street – hopefully find a cab along the way," suggested Cameron.

"Sounds like a plan," agreed Shona.

They walked along the pavement in Rose Street saying very little, just happily cuddling into one another occasionally kissing or rubbing noses. They looked like sixteen year olds dating for the first time. Cameron was as happy as he could ever remember being. He couldn't get over the fact that he had the most beautiful woman in the world on his arm. What a night.

They crossed Rose Street at the traffic lights and turned the corner into Frederick Street.

The pavements were empty here and as they wandered down towards Prince's Street they had a clear view of the road which was cordoned off because of the accident they had all witnessed the aftermath of earlier. The burned out car had been left sitting wrapped around the lamppost. There were blue and white tapes surrounding the vehicle draped between tall orange witches hats. One police vehicle was sitting up on the pavement near the black wreck and two policemen were studying marks on the road nearby and taking photographs. A large white tow truck was sitting ten metres down the road from the wreck, the driver and his mate both dosing in the front seats.

Cameron did not want to break the romantic bubble which had engulfed both Shona and himself but he couldn't help himself ask, "Did you have anything to do with Rachel?"

"I was thinking of her too Cam..." Shona replied.

"Way back in the early days when Harry was trying to get Randal to join up with NAVH's – Harry and Rachel used to wine us and dine us fairly frequently. I always thought their relationship seemed strained though. He was forever niggling her and criticising her. She was nice but didn't seem to want to be involved. Harry always seemed more interested in Belinda. I wondered if they were having an affair. Randal couldn't keep his eyes off Belinda. Harry seemed oddly happy with that. Belinda struck me as a cold, calculating bitch right from the start."

"Rachel and Harry had been living apart for at least twelve months when she died. She still lived in London and he was living at the house in the Cotswolds. As I understood it she had never even been there... They hated each other's guts by then. They loathed each other. They're relationship was toxic."

"She tried to contact me the day she died... She had something very important to discuss with me... She left 3 messages with my answer service that day wanting to set up a meeting. I assumed that she was thinking of divorcing Harry and was wanting to fish for information on him and NAVH's. She was probably wanting to get a figure on what Harry was worth. I thought she probably thought I knew lots through Randal. Randal had never discussed any financial details with me – ever. I think he had his own plans..."

"Maybe she knew other things…Maybe she had something else on her mind…"Cameron ventured.

"Like what?" Shona seemed very interested in his line of thought.

"The same day that she died she called Lydia several times too. She had something she wanted to discuss with Lydia. Lydia never got back to her either…"

"I'm lost. What are you thinking?"

"I'm worried that Rachel might have wanted to spill the beans about some of Harry and NAVH's dirty little business secrets. Maybe she knew something about Damien's suicide. It all seems too coincidental that she wanted to talk to both of you and then suddenly she dies in a car crash."

She squeezed Cameron's hand. "Oh Cameron – she was loaded up on alcohol, cocaine and amphetamines… She killed herself. She was probably very depressed. Her world was in a mess…"

Cameron said nothing. He was worried that he was shitting on what could be the greatest night of his life.

She squeezed his hand tighter. "Cameron… I think you've lost friends tragically and are hurting. You're looking for things that aren't there…"

She stopped him on the pavement and wrapped her harms around him and hugged him close. He reciprocated. They hugged for several minutes on the empty pavement. Eventually he pulled his head back to look into her face.

"Can I ask you one question? There's something that's just killing me at the moment?"

"Of course you can Cam…"

"Why are you letting Harry parade you around as if he owns you? I don't understand."

She continued to look directly at him and paused a few seconds before answering.

"As I said a minute ago Randal never discussed anything about NAVH's with me. I have no idea about their finances or what they're worth. When Randal left - he left me paying the mortgage, looking after the kids, no money in the bank, no job. The bastard left me penniless and desperate. Randal owes me big style. I sacrificed my job, my life to bring up his kids… our kids…The best years of my life I gave up so that he could become a wonder vet, so that he could cruise around in intellectual circles looking like a god. Then I went along with his "Dream for bettering private veterinary practice as we know it". He used all the superannuation and remortgaged the house to buy a slice of NAVH's. Then after the best part of thirty years he drops me like a rock. Not quietly – in front of the whole veterinary world and within moments he's shacked up with a psycho woman who he's been shagging for years behind my back. Everyone knew about it but me. Everyone knows about it. Everyone thinks that I am soft and weak and useless…"

"Harry seems to have the hots for me. I don't understand why. But I've decided to use it. If I can get close enough to Harry I might get close enough to access NAVH's finances. Not that I expect Harry to divulge much, but he might give me clues or give me ideas where I can look. I understand the world is watching and they all think I'm mad. I don't give a shit any more. They'll all understand when I take Randal to the cleaners. They'll all know that I played the pair of them…"

She looked calmly into Cameron's eyes. She was a woman on a mission.

Cameron spoke quietly. "Shona. You are the nicest, most beautiful being on the planet… But you're playing with fire… I think these bastards are dangerous. You think you're playing them… Believe me – they are playing you too. They are not stupid. They are luring you…baiting you… They are evil pricks. Everything they do is for a reason. Harry is the devil incarnate… Give him a wide berth… Leave it alone. You're too close. You'll get burned. Money isn't everything. You've got your health and you're kids and you are so, so beautiful. Please…Leave it alone…"

They looked at each other for a long time. They both had their own mental torments. They both had their demons to deal with.

She kissed him tenderly on the lips and spoke softly. "Let's talk more about all this through the week. Tonight I need you. I want you more than anything else in the world. I have dreamed about holding you and loving you and being with you for years. You have been my escape. In my head I have loved you for years. Even at university, even when I was with Randal – uni, engaged, married... I have always loved you inside my head. Dreaming of you has kept me sane..."

Cameron stared at her in disbelief. The most beautiful woman in the world had been in love with him since they first met and he never knew. He continued to stare.

She kissed him again. Softly. On the lips. He smiled widely and hugged her close. He wasn't sure what to say. Eventually some words crept out.

"You are the most beautiful thing in creation...and I've known that for thirty years."

Chapter 19

As they turned into Prince's Street there seemed to be cabs everywhere. Within a few seconds they were climbing into the back of a big black "Hackney" carriage. The cabbie, a young Pakistani chap with a fantastic Pakistani-Scottish accent, gave up on his tourist banter within a minute or so as the couple in the back snuggled up close and seemed to be oblivious to his enthusiasm for this wonderful city and his new home country.

Cameron loved the feel of the beautiful woman wrapped around him on the back seat of the cab. Her arms hugged him tight and she had buried her head against his chest. Her perfume was sublime. The warmth of her body continued to delight him. However his thoughts wandered.

His brain was juggling the evening's latest revelations. Rachel had had information for Lydia. She also had had information for Shona. She had died with Harry watching... Cameron was thinking that Harry probably knew she was going to talk to them both... He knew everything else. Lydia thought that Harry had access to her e-mails... Maybe he had access to all their e-mails... Maybe he knew exactly what Rachel wanted to tell them both... Harry and Rachel had been living apart for at least 12 months – they hated each other's guts... Cameron could hear John Davidson's words again and again. "It almost killed him. Poor Harry... And now he lives knowing she was alive in the wreck of the car and he couldn't get her out. He watched while she died." Poor Harry... Poor fucking Harry my arse... Lydia's voice then took over, "There are no coincidences... Join the dots..."

Cameron's thoughts were brought back to the inside of the "Hackney" as Shona lifted her head and smiled at him. "Are you OK? You've gone awfully quiet..."

"Sorry gorgeous – Just trying to get my head around all the NAVH's stuff."

She grinned. "I'll give you something better to think about."

She pulled his head down and kissed him passionately on the lips. Her tongue started to explore deep inside his mouth. He thought she might swallow his tonsils. Her hand slid inside his shirt and rubbed gently across the skin of his chest playing delicately with his nipples and pulling at the matt of hair extending from his chest down his to his abdomen and beyond... An instant erection tore up inside his underpants threatening to pull out any pubic hair that got in the way of it's progress. The pain of losing a few pubes was ecstatic torture as he wriggled his hips to make way for the growth of his animal friend inside his pants... His own hand slid to caress Shona's stomach and she made small squeaking gasps as his hand slid gently along the underside of her breasts.

Cameron was lost. She was the most luscious being in the omniverse. She was soft and warm and responded wonderfully to every little touch. He thought he'd died and gone to heaven. His dick was so hard he thought it might break off.

A Pakistani-Scottish accent brought him back to the real world.

"Hey Mister... We're here... The Sheraton Hotel... Do you want to get out here?"

Both Cameron and Shona grinned and looked at the driver who was standing outside the cab with the back door held open. Neither of them had realised they'd arrived at their destination. Neither of them knew how long the driver had been trying to persuade them to get out of his vehicle. He was probably worried they were going to go the whole way on the back seat.

"Sorry mate. Didn't realise we were here already." Cameron grinned sheepishly at the cabby.

As they both climbed out Shona would not make eye contact with the cabbie and Cameron realised that her skin had gone a delicious pink colour. She was blushing intensely.

Cameron slapped a twenty pound note in the cabby's hand. As he leaned into the front seat to get change Cameron said, "Don't worry about change mate. Thank you very much for the ride."

The cabby beamed at Cameron, "Thank you very much sir. I hope you have a nice night."

Cameron turned and put an arm around Shona and as they walked to the front door of the hotel they both burst into hysterical laughter. Tears were leaking from the corners of Shona's eyes. Cameron's whole frame was vibrating as he guffawed noisily.

They entered the hotel still laughing and as they crossed to foyer towards the lifts a familiar face appeared at the Concierge's desk. Ramone waved to them both enthusiastically.

"Good evening Mr Cameron. I hope you have had a good night."

"Thanks Ramone. We've had a great night. How did you get on with the Japanese ladies earlier on...Any luck?"

"Ramone grinned. No luck Mr Cameron...But they are here for seven nights..."

Cameron grinned at the young Spaniard who continued.

"Tonight the score is - Barcelona nil...Glasgow Celtic 10"

Cameron cracked up and Shona looked at him enquiringly. Cameron just shook his head and grinned at her. They were still heading liftwards when Ramone jogged around from behind the desk and handed Cameron a small hotel card.

"My personal telephone number is on the back. If you need anything at all while you're here feel free to ring...Any time."

Cameron grinned at his new mate. "Thank you Ramone. You are a true gentleman..."

Ramone nodded and quietly said, "Goodnight Sir, Goodnight Madame." He then turned and jogged back towards the concierge desk. Cameron and Shona grinned at each other as he retreated to his station.

They snuggled together in the lift and watched the floor numbers climb through G to 4 on the small screen on the digital pad beside the lift doors. Neither of them talked as Shona held Cameron's hand and led him past room 444 and thirty metres further down the corridor to room 467. Cameron was excited. He didn't know what to say. He didn't want to say anything that could change the course of events that was unfolding for him. Shona produced her door card and swiped it. She quietly opened the door and led him through. Dim light came from the room within. As the door slid quietly closed behind him he was engulfed if beautiful warm woman. She wrapped her arms around his neck and pulled his face down to hers and kissed him ravenously.

They kissed each other's mouths and eyes and faces. Her tongue once again explored the depths of his mouth. He returned the favour and rediscovered the softness of her lips and her beautiful exciting taste. He felt her hands tearing his shirttail form inside his trousers then pulling him against her as her hands gently massaged every single inch of his back under his shirt. Her hands travelled around to the front of his chest and she scratched gently through his chest hair and once again rubbed his nipples.

His own hands moved gently up and down her back. The bare skin of her shoulders, neck and upper back was a soft delight to touch. He moved his hands slowly south till they held her gorgeous bum cheeks. He squeezed her bum firmly and pulled her tightly against him. She did not resist in the slightest and pushed against him enthusiastically. They ground their hips together and his huge erection pushed hard into her softness. He thought he might lose it completely as she pushed her naughty bits firmly against his crotch.

Cameron was in heaven. He was also ecstatic and relieved. He was worried that after a couple of bottles of champagne and a dozen pints of lager that his friend in his pants might not want to perform. His stiffy was fantastic – rock hard and straining at the bit – a real diamond cutter. His next worry would be not to explode before the ultimate moment. She was grinding against him ridiculously wonderfully.

He slid his hands around her body and gently fondled the most wonderful breasts in history. She gasped and whimpered softly. Her breathing had sped up and she responded to his touch by pushing against him even more forcibly. He was having a religious moment. These breasts were the stuff of dreams – Soft and firm and wonderfully made. He could feel her erect nipples pushing into his fingers through her dress.

He was suddenly aware that her hand had dropped to his groin and she was rubbing his stiffy through his trousers. It felt divine. She rubbed harder and harder and then within an instant she slid her hand into his pants and squeezed his erection firmly. Her touch was electric. He thought he might die. My god it was wonderful. She would not let go. She pulled and squeezed and pulled and squeezed until he thought he was going to orgasm there and then.

He had to get into her dress. His hands moved around to the zip low between her shoulder blades. The zip was tiny. He could not get a hold of it properly and when he did it seemed jammed. He fumbled with the zip for and eternity while Shona unbuckled his trousers and undid the zip and let his trouser fall to his ankles. Then both hands were in his underpants massaging and pulling on his dick. My god...Oh my god...Within a few seconds she had unbuttoned his shirt, pulled it off his shoulders and dropped it on the floor also.

"I bet you think I'm terrible," she whispered as she continued her massage down under.

"No I think you are absolutely wonderful..." Cameron gasped in reply.

In the next few moments Shona disappeared from Cameron's sight and then...Oh my God...he felt the most wonderful sensations as the top of his best friend disappeared into her soft, wet mouth. The feelings were excruciatingly wonderful. His body had moved to another planet. The feelings were magnificent. Her teeth and her tongue teased him but she gripped him tightly so that he could not explode. He gasped and groaned for several minutes and wound his fingers through her hair as she gave him the most immense pleasure.

She stood up again, looking into his eyes grinning like the cat who'd got the cream.

"I've dreamed of doing that for years..."

She turned to face away from him and her hands reached over her head and undid the zip on the back of her dress and slid it down the first two or three inches. Cameron kissed the back of her neck and slid the zip all the way down to her bum. She shrugged and wiggled her shoulders and the dress fell fluidly to the floor. She now wore only beautiful ivory coloured panties and bra. Cameron closed the gap between them and his excited member rubbed her bum cheeks through her undies and pushed into the small of her back. He reached around and cupped her breasts in his hands. They filled his hands and were straining against the delicate fabric of her bra. They were the most beautiful things he had ever touched. He was fascinated. They were wonderful.

Shona's hands returned to her back and she unhooked her bra-strap and let the bra fall to the floor with her dress. Cameron was in heaven. He caressed Shona's breasts and listened to her groan and gasp. When he touched her nipples her whole body arched and stiffened. Cameron loved how she responded to his every touch. He kissed her neck and playfully bit her shoulders. Her groans got louder. Cameron dropped his hand to her knickers and gently pushed the elastic waistband down over her hips. They joined her bra and dress under their feet. She reached over her shoulder and pulled his face to hers and when their mouths met he thought she might eat him. She kissed him hungrily and would not stop. His hands caressed her stomach and then slowly descended to explore the holy land. As he touched her beautifully manicured strip of short pubic hair she cried out – "Oh my God – don't stop". He let his hand descend further and found that she was extremely moist and inviting. She wriggled around excitedly as he explored delicately. Her body started to vibrate gently.

She turned to face him and pushed him back into the room towards the huge double bed. She was grinning but her eyes seemed glazed. The bedroom was illuminated by both bedside lamps and for the first time Cameron could see her whole delicious naked body. She was beautiful. Beautiful beyond belief. She pushed him back onto the bed and he dragged her down on top of him. They wriggled up until Cameron's head lay on the pillows. She was on all fours over the top of him staring into his face. He kissed her gently on the lips and then slid gently underneath her kissing her soft delicious skin as he went. When he arrived at her breasts he cupped them in his hands gently and massaged them softly. She whimpered quietly and he raised his head and kissed her breasts and licked her beautiful nipples. She cried out wildly – "Oh my God...Oh my God..." She collapsed on top of him and he was engulfed in wonderful soft breasts. For a moment he thought he might suffocate – his brain told him it would be the most wonderful way to go. Within a couple of seconds Shona rolled off allowing him to breathe again. She slid several inches down the bed and then lay directly on top of him.

It felt wonderful. She was staring into his eyes. Her breasts were flattened against his chest and his tireless erection was nestling against her lovely trimmed bush. She ground her hips slowly against him. Her smile widened.

She stooped and whispered in his ear, "You're absolutely gorgeous...But I really do need to go have a pee..." The both laughed and Cameron stared at her, hypnotised, as she climbed from the bed and disappeared into the bathroom.

He was besotted. She was absolutely beautiful. As he listened to her doing girly things in the bathroom he wondered if this would be the only time ever. When this one night was over would it be back to Shona baiting Harry and then him off back to Australia to sort out his own sad love life... His best friend had deflated slightly...Shit what a thought. He had to make the most of tonight. He could treasure the night forever. Maybe this was the start of a whole new life... Maybe... What if this was the one and only night in his life he was to sleep with the most gorgeous woman he'd ever met?

In an instant he was off the bed and fumbling through his trousers. He found his mobile and jumped straight back on the bed. He flicked to Camera and selected video. His good conscience was screaming, "Don't be ridiculous Cam..." The alcohol affected conscience stated matter-of-factly "This might be the only night in your whole life..." As his consciences duelled in his head he heard movement in the bathroom next door and lights flickered as doors opened and shut. For a fleeting second he imagined that the light flickering had come from the main door to the room but it couldn't have and Shona seemed to be having problems with the bathroom door. In a split second he hit the on switch on the video screen and placed the phone against the bedside lamp stand looking back over the whole room. His brain screamed, "You can't do that you fucking scum bag." The voices in his head evaporated quickly as the most glorious site of a naked Shona Hollingsworth materialised in the arc of light at the end of the bed.

She stood for a moment and smiled before climbing back onto the bed.

Cameron smiled back wondering if she'd noticed the phone. She grinned. Cameron relaxed. His erection grew to mammoth proportions and he thought it had set like concrete. It was so huge and hard it was painful.

Shona climbed onto the bed and knelt beside him. Her left hand gently stroked his engorged member.

"I do believe you're happy to see me again." She laughed.

"I'm absolutely delighted to see you." Cameron returned quietly watching her hand on his friend.

She massaged his member softly for several minutes and made Cameron gasp and squirm. She laughed and continued her fun. Eventually she climbed on top of him and put the tip only, just into her soft wet place. Cameron groaned. Slowly she started moving her hips... Initially around and around, then backwards and forwards, and as she did, she slowly slid down his shaft until it completely disappeared and their pelvises ground together.

Shona groaned quietly and let out little ecstatic gasps as she took control and dictated rate and rhythm. Cameron groaned happily and reached up and massaged her gorgeous breasts. Shona groaned louder and more constantly and bent lower towards him so that her breasts were more easily reached.

They ground together for several long minutes and the groaning became louder and more constant. Cameron was afraid he would explode too soon the sensations were so unbearably wonderful. He desperately did not want to go off before Shona had had a wonderful time too.

He closed his eyes and concentrated on staying as long as possible. My god he was so close...So close... Shona's body slowly started vibrating. The vibrations started in her pelvis and emanated out spreading through her body and limbs. The vibrations accelerated when their bodies were closest together, their pubic bones grinding hard against each other.

Suddenly Cameron could feel Shona's internal muscles squeezing around his manhood and her gyrating was accelerating dramatically. She was crying constantly... "Oh my God...Oh my God..." Cameron's dick was going mental and suddenly he just couldn't hold on any longer. He thrust hard and fast into Shona as his wild trouser friend went absolutely crazy. He pumped and pumped and pumped and suddenly he was exploding inside her. His orgasm was so long and intense he thought he might black out. The sensations were like nothing he'd ever encountered before. He was truly in heaven. At the same time Shona was screaming ecstatically and bouncing around on top of him like a woman possessed. Her body was vibrating and shaking all over. She was lost in her own orgasmic frenzy.

Suddenly the screaming stopped and was replaced by hoarse wheezing gasps. Cameron felt warm fluid showering onto his face and chest and Shona collapsed on top of him writhing uncontrollably. The wheezing noise sounded wet and horrible and the fluid kept pouring onto his chest and splashing up onto his face. He couldn't understand what was happening. Was she vomiting? Was she having a fit? His eyes flew open. Panic messages were flying though his brain. Was she OK? What the fuck was happening? In the first few seconds he could see nothing apart from her twitching body on top of his. Suddenly she was a dead weight. Her arms and legs were flailing around smashing into both him and the bed. She rolled to his left side and he couldn't understand what was happening – his brain could see what was in front of him but it could not be real.

Shona was covered in bright red blood. The blood was spraying from her throat like water from a fire hose. A huge slash across her throat was gaping wide open from ear to ear just below her chin. The wet gasping wheezes were coming from a gaping trachea which was clogging with bright red blood and purple clots. As she flailed around on the bed her arms were grabbing at him and her face and eyes were searching his face in sheer terror. Blood was flying everywhere. Cameron couldn't understand. She was still trying to hold him but the lower half of her body slid off the edge of the bed pulling the rest of her behind. Cameron heard her head hit the floor with a dull thud as he desperately tried to stop her from falling. What the fuck... He jumped from the bed and knelt over the top of her. She was now staring at the ceiling with vague, unseeing eyes.

"Shona, Shona stay with me..." Cameron begged. He grabbed handfuls of sheets off the bed and pushed them into her gaping throat to try and staunch the bleeding. His brain was screaming in disbelief. He pushed more and more sheets into the wound but the blood still oozed through and onto the floor where it was forming a red/purple halo around her head. His brain was trying to cope – Airway, breathing, circulation – emergency procedures – ABC... Her airway was clogged with blood and every time he tried to clear it she bled more. He tried and tried to clear her gaping trachea. Blood gushed from inside both edges of the gaping hole in her throat. He was focussed on stopping the bleeding and maintaining an airway but neither was happening. He manically tried to clear the blood from her trachea and push firmly against ruptured blood vessels.

"Shona, Shona...Hang on... I'll get and ambulance... Can you hold the sheets up here?" He lifted her limp arms and attempted to get her to hold the sheets onto the haemorrhaging sites on her throat. She would not help him. He talked to her for a long time and frantically cleared her airways. Eventually after several long excruciating minutes he stopped and looked directly at what lay in front of him. He wiped tears from his eyes.

Shona's eyes were dull...Her corneas looked rubbery, her pupils were dilated. Her skin was whiter than white. There were no more gasps or wheezes. He realised that she had not breathed for several minutes. The bleeding from the gaping wound in her throat had stopped. The blood on the floor around her head was congealed and dark red black. There were no flailing arms or legs. She was still and quiet. His hand moved to the left side of her chest where he thought he should feel a heartbeat. He stayed there for several more endless minutes and felt nothing.

Cameron slumped against the bed. He was stunned. He was in shock. He couldn't understand. He was dreaming. This had not happened. This was absurd. He was about to wake up.

He sat and stared at Shona.

He crouched over her again and shook her arms...
"Shona...Shona... Wake up... Wake up..."

He stared at her for more long minutes and suddenly felt sick. He couldn't move away. He couldn't get up. He crouched over Shona's flaccid body and vomited all over the blood stained floor and across her ivory white legs. He vomited and retched. Food and fluid came out both his mouth and nose and stinging tears spilled from his eyes and ran down his face to mingle with the vomit. Once there was nothing left to vomit, he dry retched for several more agonising minutes until his whole body ached. He felt faint and the room started spinning. He managed to sit up with his back against the bed. He closed his eyes and screamed inside his head.

Chapter 20

Cameron sat naked on the floor, his back against the bed, his blood covered knees pulled up tight against himself. He hugged his knees and slowly rocked backwards and forwards. His arms were covered in dark purple blood. Clots clung to the hair on his forearms. His chest had bloody handprints dragged across it. Stringy clots hung in the hair there. He had dried blood smeared all over his thighs and cold, sticky blood squelched in the creases of his groin as he rocked. The floor below him was wet and stained – a mixture of blood and vomit. His feet and buttocks were lost in the mess on the floor. Shona's lifeless body lay grotesquely beside him staring blindly at the ceiling, the horrific wound in her throat gaping like a second screaming mouth. Her body had somehow shrunk. She was tiny. Her translucent white skin was stained with purple black blood which covered most of her body and spread around her torso and crept under the bed and onto the nearby skirting boards. The wall at the bedhead had been sprayed by blood fountains. Arcs of red covered the wall with bizarre red frills underneath where the blood had tried to drip downwards. In places rivulets had run down to pool above the skirting board and then dribble onto the floor merging with the huge lake of blood there. Cameron moaned quietly as he rocked. He wasn't here. He couldn't be here. Here was worse than hell.

Over the next half hour Cameron could not force himself to open his eyes. He refused to believe what he had just witnessed. He did not want to confirm the reality of this horrific nightmare.

Eventually his mind cleared. Rational thinking returned. He had to move. He had to corroborate his worst thoughts... He had to contact the police... Shona could not be allowed to lie there any longer... She deserved respect... She could not be left in such a hellish state.

He steeled himself and opened his eyes. The sight he beheld was worse than horrendous. The most beautiful woman he had ever met was unrecognisable. She did not look like a person any more. There was a tiny fragile figure lying in a pool of blood. She looked like a broken doll – her limbs spread on the floor at all the wrong angles. Her head seemed to be barely attached to her body. Her eyes were blank. Nobody lived there anymore.

Cameron felt remarkably calm. He stared at the most beautiful woman in the world for several long moments and then slowly climbed to his feet. He had to call the police. He had to call someone. He sat heavily on the edge of the bed and tried to collect his thoughts.

If he called the police they would surely believe that he had murdered her. He was covered in her blood. But he hadn't murdered her. They would be able to work it out...But... What the fuck had happened? Jesus Christ – one minute he was shagging her – the next minute she was bleeding to death with her throat sliced open. How the fuck did that work? He tried to re live his last few seconds of passion with Shona in his mind...It had been fantastic they were both going crazy and then suddenly out of the blue she collapses on top of him bleeding like a stuck pig... Fucking Hell...Fucking, Fucking Hell... What the hell had happened?

There had to be someone else in the room. Now you're really away with the fairies Cambo.

There had to be somebody else in the room... You're fucking dreaming mate...

Cameron turned slowly and looked towards the bedside lamp on the other side of the bed. His mobile phone sat where he'd left it looking back across the whole room...He stared at it quietly. He rose and walked around the bed and picked it up. The phone was still taking a video recording...

He was scared to touch it. He was scared to know if it had been witness to Shona's horrific death. He was scared that if he hit the wrong button then any recording could be lost forever.

His hands were shaking as he paused the video. He hit the save option. The video had been stored in his photo collection. He punched the screen a few times and the video appeared ready to play. Duration – 47 minutes and 11 seconds... Bloody long video... He noted that the battery was getting fairly low. He stared at the screen realising that he had been smearing blood all over it. He had to see this now. He hit the play button.

The view of the room was great. The middle of the bed was in the centre of the screen. You couldn't quite see Cam's head but there was a very good view of his rampant member and Shona standing at the end of the bed smiling. She climbed onto the bed and started pulling his dick until it was the size of Apollo 10... As she climbed on board Cameron suddenly felt sick again. He paused the clip and took several deep breaths. When he was composed again he slid the cursor along the video timeline and advanced in time until it looked like they were just about to climax. He hit play.

Shona's voice screamed from the phone, " Oh my God , Oh my God," and she bounced around on top of Cameron while his body shuddered underneath her. Within moments she was vibrating uncontrollably on top of him. Cameron's eyes squinted at the small screen. Something had changed. A dark shape had moved within the shadows at the foot of the bed. He paused the video and then continued in slow motion – frame by frame. Shona's screams dropped several octaves and Cameron stared in disbelief as a hand wielding a scalpel which glinted in the light from the bedside lamps suddenly appeared under her chin. Cameron was aware that another hand had grabbed into her hair and pulled her head violently backwards. In the same instant the blade sliced through her throat and crazy fountains of blood erupted from the wound.

Cameron was dry retching again but could not take his eyes from the screen. Shona's assailant threw her forward on top of Cameron where she wheezed and choked and shook violently.

As Cameron continued to watch with sickening revulsion he saw the dark shape of Shona's attacker turn and head for the door of the room. Cameron could hardly breathe. He could hear his heart beating erratically within his chest. Time had slowed. He stood stock still – staring at the small screen. He paused the video and replayed the last few frames...Again and again. He froze the picture at the very moment that Shona was thrown down on top of him and stared at the face just outside the arc of light. It was not well lit but it didn't have to be. He felt repulsed. He felt sickened. He felt mad. The unmistakable face of Harry Ainsworth was leering at them both before turning and disappearing into the darkness.

Chapter 21

Cameron knew he should telephone the police immediately. He knew he should... But deep primordial instincts took over. His thoughts were cold and calculating.

He needed revenge for the atrocity which had just occurred... For all the atrocities which Harry had committed. Cameron now was sure that Harry had killed both Damien and Rachel. Harry had raped Lydia. He had killed Shona in the most horrific way imaginable. Harry was abusing the whole world. How many other deaths or "suicides" was Harry involved in? How many other people was he blackmailing? Manipulating? Playing god with... Harry had actually evolved to become the devil himself... No conscience. No remorse. Unfeeling. Capable of anything to reach his goals... Cameron was going to find Harry and make him suffer... Suffer like he had never imagined... The police could have him afterwards if he was still alive... Harry was about to wish that he had never been born.

Cameron searched the floor of the room for his clothes. Bizarrely they had vanished...His wallet and it's contents were strewn across the floor – cards and loose change everywhere but no clothes... They were not on the floor where they had dropped...Not kicked under the bed or any other furniture. His shoes and socks were haphazardly strewn across the floor between the door of   the room and the bathroom door but his clothes were nowhere. What the fuck. He opened the bathroom door and flicked on the light. His eyes were immediately drawn to small black trail of blood spots which led across the tiled floor to the sink. He stared into the sink. A blood covered Captain Brand scalpel handle with blade attached lay in the bottom of the sink. The bastard. The fucking bastard. Cameron stopped short of picking it up. He stood by the sink and stared at it. He toyed with the idea of using it on Harry. Maybe that would be poetic justice...Remove his balls...Maybe chop off his dick...Maybe ram it up his arse... With no emotion Cameron conjured up visions of chopping Harry up with the scalpel... Making him scream and beg for mercy...

He was wasting time. He wanted to find Harry fast. Maybe Harry would alert the police that something was amiss in Room 467... He was sure that Harry would be setting him up for Shona's murder.

He glanced in the mirror and did not recognise himself. A naked man, painted in blood looked back at him. He had blood in his hair, around his eyes and caked around his chin. His whole body was streaked with purple and black blood stains. There were even blood clots matted in his pubes. He realised that the lower half of his body was also covered in dry puke.

No clothes in the bathroom but he could smell the lovely smell of Shona and her perfume lingering in the air. He stood and inhaled deeply. He would never smell that smell again.

He climbed into the bath tub and hit the tap to switch the shower on. Almost immediately he was blasted by a jet of freezing water. He stood without flinching and let the cold water pummel his body. The water cascading into the bath and running down the plughole was the colour of red wine. He closed his eyes and stood under the water for several minutes clearing his thoughts and contemplating his next move. He was still covered in blood when he opened his eyes. He turned the tap to hot and grabbed a face washer and a bar of soap and scrubbed till he was reasonably clean. Small blood clots still held to the hairs on his arms and legs and also in his crotch. When he pulled them from his skin they clung stubbornly to the hairs and were damned painful to try and remove. For a moment he was back in Australia in the shower at home. He could spend hours picking blood clots and fibrin from the hairs on his arms after a difficult calving or after a bovine caesarean. No time for that now. As long as he got the worst off. He was going to have to walk through the hotel to find Harry. If he was covered in blood Security would probably grab him before he'd gone even a short way. He thought he might be presentable now. He switched off the shower and climbed out of the bath. He grabbed a towel and started drying himself. As he stared at the guy in the mirror again he realised that he looked a lot cleaner but not very healthy. His eyes had sunk back into black holes in his head, his lips were swollen and cracked and there were still flecks of blood in both of his ears. He lifted the towel to wipe his ears and realised that the thick white bath towel was now mostly pink with small blood clots caught in the dense thread. Fuck. That would have to do.

He walked back out into the small hallway between the main door and the bathroom and opened the wardrobe. He pulled a large white dressing gown off a coat hanger and climbed into it. He tied the cotton belt of the gown tightly around him.

He walked back into the main room and gathered his wallet and cards from the floor. He kept his room key card separate and packed the rest back in the wallet. He put the wallet in one of the deep pockets of the dressing gown alongside the room card. He picked up his phone and looked at it. He picked up a handful of sheet from the war torn bed and wiped the phone clean.

Still one bar of battery. He started punching icons on the screen.

He reached back into the dressing gown pocket and pulled out his wallet. He thumbed through the stack of cards which lived there until he found the card that Ramone had given him a couple of hours earlier.

He composed a text to Logan Bloomsberry, Mick O'Reilly , Peter McEwan and Ramone –

Please DONOT, I repeat DONOT open the video. Tragedy has struck. Shona has been killed. DONOT open the video. Keep the video as evidence. In a moment I'm going to phone you all on a conference call. Please answer the phone but DONOT speak. The phone will be with me while I try to get a confession from a killer. Please listen carefully but DONOT try to intervene. When I have the confession the police will be called. He attached the video and hit the send button.

He then took a minute and punched more icons on his phone. He set up the phone for his conference call to the four people he had just messaged. He pocketed the phone with his wallet.

He then returned to the bathroom and picked up a small hand towel. He carefully picked the blood covered scalpel, with the blade still attached, from the sink. He wrapped it in the hand towel and placed it carefully in the other empty pocket of the dressing gown.

He then returned to the bedroom and stopped near the foot of the bed. He forlornly looked at the remains of the most gorgeous Shona Hollingsworth. She was unrecognisable. Last night she had been full of the joys of life - effervescent, warm, sexy, voluptuous and vital... Now... This was not her... She was somewhere else...She did not deserve this... This was a tragedy...An absolute atrocity...

Cameron turned into the small hallway and opened the main door.

As he exited the room he whispered to himself...and to Shona.., "He's going to die. Harry Ainsley is going to die. But before he does he's going to beg for forgiveness for every sin he's ever committed..."

Chapter 22

Cameron walked quickly down the hallway towards his room. His plan was to get into some clothes and then call Harry and bait him into a meeting. He was flying blind but if he had witnesses to his meeting with Harry on the other end of his phone they would hear Harry explaining his guilt or non-guilt. Cameron thought that if he gave him enough rope he might hang himself. He would challenge Harry with his thoughts about the whole NAVH's set-up, blackmail, fraud and murder. His best ammunition would be the video. He would have to confess. The video was surely already in the safe hands of his friends. Once Harry had confessed, Cameron had decided to switch off the phone and deliver retribution personally to Harry for his three lost friends. The scalpel played a large part in his plan for retribution and if Harry failed to confess it could also help persuade him to deliver the truth.

Cameron reached room 444 and inserted his key card into the slot above the door handle. A small green light shone from just above the slot momentarily and he depressed the handle and quietly opened the door. When the door was just open enough for him to slide through he quickly entered and pushed the door closed behind him. It was pitch black in the room. There was no light from the window. No hint of Edinburgh Castle illuminated high on its ancient rock. Housekeeping must have prepared the room for night. These thoughts flew through his brain in a microsecond and then a hellish driving pain smashed him in the side of his head. He fell heavily against the wall and suddenly there were two bodies on top of him hitting him in the guts and chest and dragging him to the floor. He attempted to cry out but his face was forced excruciatingly into the hallway carpet. More driving forces belted the wind out of him as he felt fists and knees hammer into his back and chest. Another savage blow struck the other side of his head and he fought to stay conscious. It would have been easy to give in to the enveloping dark but he had to stay with it.

His head was wrenched backwards and as he tried to cry out a hard, broad leather strap was pulled into his mouth and fastened tightly behind his head. His nose was bleeding and suddenly breathing was restricted drastically as the leather strap bit into his cheeks and prevented him from breathing through his mouth. His arms were dragged behind his back and fastened together viciously with another hard leather strap. He lay face down on the hard floor while his 2 assailants continued to kick him in the ribs and abdomen. He tried to twist and kick at them with his bare feet but in an instant his ankles were shackled with more leather strapping and pulled high up behind his back and attached to the bindings around his wrists. The position was excruciatingly painful to hold but he had no choice. He was pushed over onto his right side and pain shot up his right arm as his elbow hit the floor and the leather bindings tore at his wrists. He could not move. He could not see. He could hear heavy breathing back inside the room but there were no words. He tried to cry out but little or no sound escaped from his gagged mouth.

After several interminable seconds he was pulled back onto his stomach. He was then lifted by his arms and carried into the main bedroom and dropped face down on the side of the large double bed he remembered from earlier in the day. One of his assailants backed off but he could hear the other crouching down by the side of the bed and breathing very close to his face.

A soft click and the bedside lamp illuminated the room. The emotionless face of Harry Ainsley stared at him from less than 6 inches away. He stared at Cameron as if seeing him for the first time. He did not speak. He stared coldly for a very long couple of minutes. He was crouched on his haunches and leaning over onto the bed. Cameron could smell his sweet minty breath and a hint of his expensive cologne. His eyes were staring at some point in the back of Cameron's head.

Eventually Harry seemed to focus on Cameron's face. His expression didn't change. He quietly stated, "You haven't opened your e-mails since you got off the plane..."

There was a long pause while Harry continued to study Cameron's face.

He then continued, "Your wife sent you this video..."

He pulled a computer tablet off the bedside table and place it in front of Cameron's face so that he could see the screen easily.

He started a video playing and Cameron stared at the screen. The face of Peter Goldsmith, owner of the local chemist shop back in Aiden Falls in the Blue Mountains, was grinning at the camera and giving the thumbs up. He was taking a selfie. As he moved the camera away from his face you could see that he was naked and that there was a blonde woman sucking his dick. The camera stayed on the blonde woman's head as it bobbed up and down causing Peter to gasp with pleasure.

A sickening feeling started in Cameron's guts. He did not want to watch the rest of the video. He turned his face away but Harry grabbed him by the hair and twisted his head so that he was forced to look directly at the screen. He closed his eyes but Harry stood up and held his head with his fingers hooked under his upper eyelids and forced his face towards the screen. Cameron groaned and choked and coughed. As the video continued in front of him he saw his wife Alison briefly let go of Peter's dick and wave provocatively at the camera. She was completely naked and wiggled her gorgeous little boobs for Peter's benefit. The camera moved close in and her boobs filled the screen for several seconds. Both Peter and Alison were laughing loudly.

Cameron writhed painfully on the bed trying to escape the vision but the second unseen assailant pushed down heavily on him from behind. He was going nowhere.

The video continued for several minutes showing Peter and Alison in various innovative shagging positions and finished with them both lying spent on a bed, lathered in sweat and grinning inanely.

Cameron fought hard to stop vomiting. The sharp acid taste of vomitus filled the back of his throat. His brain was screaming. He could not unsee the sickening vision he had just witnessed. How long had this been going on? Why the fuck Peter fucking Goldsmith? Was he the only one? Oh fuck...Oh fuck... Did everybody else in the world know except him?

The video had been finished for several seconds when Harry asked, "So what's he got that you haven't Cam?"

Cameron tried to spit at him despite the gag and only managed to cause himself to choke more and restrict his breathing further.

Harry continued in the same quiet voice with the slimy, southern, posh English accent.

"When the police check your browsing history they'll find that you opened the video attachment sent by Alison at 17:02 this evening. You then downloaded it to your laptop and watched it 4 times before heading out to join your buddies... That's all thanks to Belinda our IT guru. She can access any computer in the world if it's connected to a modem. She's an IT genius... Nothing's private these days."

Harry was grinning. This was the first time he had shown any emotion at all. He felt a warm hand cupping the left cheek of his arse and the unforgettable husky voice of Belinda broke in from close behind him, "He's right Cambo... If it's documented on a computer anywhere I'll find it... You were a real let-down over the last few months. Your in-box is the most boring box I've ever been in... No pun intended."

Harry's eyes were sparkling and twinkling now. He seemed quite animated. He continued.

"So you watched the video again and again and it broke your heart you poor thing. It sent you over the edge and you lost control altogether this evening and murdered Shona in cold blood."

"Awful... Just awful..." Belinda was starting to get in on the act now.

"Everyone saw you flirting all night with Shona...and your DNA is splattered all over that room including deep inside her beautiful little manicured love haven. You're fucked Cam. You're going to be done for murder... Double murder actually..."

Belinda leaned over from the far side of the bed and grabbed a handful of Cameron's hair. She dragged his head across towards her and turned it so that he could see the other side of the huge double bed. The temperature of Cameron's soul dropped to a new low. He stared in disbelief.

Lying naked on the other side of the bed was Lydia. Face down with a couple of pillows under her stomach raising her bottom up in the air. She was bound and gagged just like Cameron. Her skin was white, almost blue. Her lips were blue tinged. Her eyes were open and unblinking. She was barely breathing. Cameron could just make out extremely shallow slow respiratory movements with long periods of no activity at all.

Belinda dragged him down the bed by his ankles till his head was just below Lydia's bum. A small trickle of dried blood sat low in the crease between her bum cheeks. Her buttocks were bruised blue and purple.

"And guess what Cam. Your DNA's all over Lydia's rear end already," continued Harry. "I just happened to find your undies earlier this evening and do you know you'd leaked a whole pile of sprog onto them before shagging Shona. Most of it is now packed deep between Lydia's bum cheeks. My god your DNA gets around... I did have a wee crack at her arse earlier in the evening but I wore a condom and I always shave my pubes these days...So no signs of Uncle Harry anywhere. It was really snug in there too. I think the stitch up job she had after last time made her tighter than before... It was rather nice."

"Unfortunately the hotel staff are going to find you both sadly passed away from heroin overdoses in the morning – both here in the same room. She's not dead yet but she's getting very close. We'll give you a big hit-up in a minute or two... It'll be a nice way to go. Kinky sex followed by a heroin overdose. I could think of a lot worse ways to go."

Cameron's mind was numb. Harry had shagged Lydia again and traumatised her badly. She was dying on the bed in front of them and both Harry and Belinda were chatting away like it was just another day at the office. They were now about to give him a heroin overdose also. He was to die with Lydia during a bondage session... Fucking Hell...

"Now Cambo honey..." It was Belinda's voice. "We're going to untie your feet from your wrists so that you can sit up for a minute... Don't even think of trying anything stupid or we'll kick the absolute shit out of you and maybe kick the shit out of Lydia just for fun too. OK?"

Cameron felt pressure between his wrists and his ankles abruptly subside. He was still in great discomfort but this was infinitely better than a few seconds ago. He was dragged to the edge of the bed and then forced to stand up. Belinda then pulled him roughly over to the sofa opposite the foot of the bed and forced him to sit. His ankles were still shackled and his hands were still tied behind his back. He could only breathe through his nose and minimal exertion caused him to cough and choke.

He was facing Lydia. They were torturing them both. She looked more blue than previously, but still there was a slight rise and fall of her chest wall at least a couple of times a minute.

Harry and Belinda sat on either side of him. Harry had returned to cool stare mode. Cameron noticed that he held an aluminium baseball bat in his hand. Fuck. Belinda pulled his dressing gown off his shoulders and pushed it roughly down his back. She busied herself with drug paraphernalia on the small table beside the sofa, syringes, teaspoons, a cigarette lighter and a packet of white powder.

Harry was definitely back in zombie mode and stared unblinking at Lydia with her bruised arse high in the air. Occasionally a hint of a smile came and went.

Cameron slowly realised that his hands although tied were now very close to the scrunched up pockets of his dressing gown. If he leant forward slightly and took the pressure off his bum he could gently pull the fabric and move the pockets closer to his hands. He only had to get into his left pocket and touch the dial button on the phone and his conference call would be made to Loges, Mick, Pete and Ramone. He'd set it up after sending his text. Fuck. He could just feel the top of the phone...or the bottom...through the thick fabric. He had already set the phone on silent mode. It would make no noise...or would it? Fuck he'd never made a call on silent mode...funny that.

Belinda was preoccupied with her heroin stash and Harry was away with the fucking fairies. Cameron pulled and pulled on the dressing gown fabric. Millimetre by millimetre the pocket crept towards his fingertips. Belinda was trying to get the lighter to work. Harry was fixated by Lydia's bum. Eventually the index finger of his right hand hooked inside the corner of the pocket. He gently pulled it round towards his back. Once there he could cup the whole phone in his hand. He spun it in his fingers till it was lying upside down in his hand with the face towards his thumb. Fuck. He had to put his pin number in...by feel. He stared into space and focussed hard on the face of the phone. He pressed gently with his thumb where he thought the numbers were positioned. An imperceptible glow of light momentarily lit his pocket behind his back. No one noticed as the light in the room changed with every click of Belinda's cigarette lighter. He was in. The phone should have opened directly onto the conference call function he'd set-up. He hit where he imagined the call icon to be and within seconds he felt a tiny vibration. He carefully replaced the phone deep in the pocket and held his breath. No one deviated from their purpose. Belinda was unwrapping syringes and Harry continued to stare at the soon to be departed Lydia.

Cameron's left hand pulled the other pocket of the dressing gown slowly towards his hand and within a minute he had the handle of the Captain Brand Scalpel held tightly in his hand with the blade pointing out behind him. He kept his hand inside the pocket so as not to reveal his hidden weapon.

Belinda now had some clear frothy fluid in her syringe. She looked at it as the bubbles settled out and fitted a hypodermic needle to the end of the syringe. She turned and talked across Cameron to Harry, "OK Harry...Bye-Bye time for the lovely Cambo..."

Harry turned. His eyes twinkling again and his grin like a Cheshire Cat.

"Fantastic Darling. You are worth more money."

Belinda returned the grin and started wrapping a rubber tourniquet tightly around Cameron's upper arm. The blood vessels in his forearm began to bulge.

"Nice veins honey," Belinda whispered into Cameron's ear.

For a fleeting second Cameron thought about diving away from the sofa and attempting some form of violence on them both but Harry had risen and was holding the baseball bat against Cameron's temple and was posturing as if teeing up for a golf drive. Immediate death by bludgeoning did not appeal. He felt a prick in his left forearm and a warm sensation floated through his body. Belinda released the tourniquet and whispered, "Good Boy Cambo..."

Cameron felt a warm sensation in his groin and immediately started feeling light headed. He badly wanted to pee. Slowly the sun came out. He was surrounded by warm yellow light. He felt good...Really good. Suddenly the world was a good place.

Harry put the baseball bat on the bed and turned and looked at Harry. He smiled warmly.

"Cameron my old friend," he announced, "You've given us a good means of tidying up a couple of loose and irritating ends. We were not sure just how we were going to rid ourselves of Shona and Lydia but your arrival and your interest in both of them gave us an easy out. The stupid women were always going to get in the way of progress and that little slut Shona was only chasing a golden handshake. Well Cameron she didn't fucking deserve it."

"Randal will be eternally grateful. He's in bed with the British Ambassador to Switzerland's daughter even as we speak. He knew he'd need a good alibi so the timing is perfect."

"Lydia just wouldn't go away. We tried to keep her happy. We looked after her daughter... the dirty little whore... We've continued to pay Damien's salary directly to Lydia... but we still hear grumblings from her... I'm afraid that she had huge potential to upset the applecart at some point... If only Damien had gone along with the plan the stupid bastard... Involving the BSAVA was just fucking absurd... At least we relieved him of his misery... No more worrying about crack whore Janey and no more worrying about upsetting old ladies who can't afford his services... No more worrying for poor old Damien now..."

Harry paused and his smile grew to a huge leering grin. He continued staring into Cameron's eyes.

"...Shit did he bleed... I almost got a hard-on watching... It was spectacular... he spray-painted the whole fucking office..."

Harry paused for several seconds as he relived the grotesque event... still staring deep into Cameron's eyes.

"...And Lydia the darling had already fixed the CCTV for me... She can be such a sweetie... And don't worry about Hotel Security and CCTV. Belinda has rigged the CCTV server to fail tonight and as if by magic there's no back-up. Nobody knows we've even been here. Belinda had room service deliver champagne to my suite only 20 minutes ago. We'll be watching hotel movies all night and ordering more drinkees as we go. This is your room and the only visitor here tonight is poor Lydia."

Belinda stroked Cameron's head and then undid the gag which threatened to suffocate him. He gasped in air hungrily. He had little or no energy to attempt any escape. They both looked at him expectantly.

Cameron stammered, "Did you burn your hands setting fire to Rachel's car?"

"Very good Cambo." Harry pondered the question. "You know you're in the wrong job don't you? If the bitch hadn't tried to blackmail me she would probably still be here today..."

Harry continued.

"You know it's been a very good night Cam. We now have a video of Victor shagging Eleanor. That should be handy in acquiring his practice – It's worth about six million pounds a year you know. That could be a nice asset. But we've also got video of Belinda giving Luigi a head job in the toilet at "The Shack"... That'll give us good leverage... He's been married for 32 years and his wife is loaded...six kids and 2 grandkids who adore him... We still have more work to do there though. We're planning on taping Belinda shagging him up the arse later in the week..."

"By the way you're far smarter than we anticipated. How on earth did you know that my gorgeous friend Belinda is a she-male?"

Belinda took her cue and stood in front of Cameron rubbing her crotch. She licked her lips and the unmistakable outline of an erect penis slowly grew against her lower abdomen and pushed through the clinging material of her dress.

"How did you know Cambo?" Harry persisted.

Cameron formed his words carefully and talked quietly and slowly, "You wouldn't understand Harry – I'm Scottish..."

Harry laughed loudly delighted by the response.

There was an eruption of laughter outside the door of the room and both Harry and Belinda froze and stared towards the door.

Suddenly Cameron lunged forward off the sofa spinning as he rose and fell backwards into Belinda driving the full length of the Captains Brand scalpel deep into her abdomen from inside his robe pocket. Belinda screamed hysterically and suddenly the door to the room flew open. Ramone and Mick hurtled across the short hallway and dived on top of Harry. They all crashed to the floor with limbs flailing everywhere and the sound of painful thuds as Harry received a horrendous beating from the fit and athletic Ramone and Mick who was striking at a man he had despised for years. Harry squealed like a pig. Loges and Peter brought up the rearguard and both dived on Belinda who was screaming like a banshee. She was leaking copious amounts of blood onto the floor from under her dress. When both men hit her she dropped like a sack of spuds and her head hit the floor with a sickening thud. Belinda lay on the floor twitching. The blow to the head had knocked her senseless. Harry continued to squeal as the boys belted him repeatedly. With every fierce blow Mick uttered an expletive, "Bastard… Bastard… Prick…Murdering fucking shite…"Eventually the beating stopped and Harry was restrained and held pinned to the floor by Ramone. He whimpered softly.

Mick rose red faced and panting. He crossed the floor to where Cameron lay bound on the carpet and knelt beside him. He gasped, "You man are a fucking idiot. You could have been dead too for fuck sake…" He reached down between Cameron's ankles and slowly untied the leather bindings. When he'd untied the wrist restraints also, he gave Cameron a hand to get to his feet.

"Now sit your arse on that sofa till we get you some medical attention," Mick insisted.

Cameron ignored Mick and walked slowly across the floor and drove his foot as hard as he could into Harry's groin. Harry gasped and cried loudly. The boys stood and watched while Cameron repeated the insult. He then knelt and whispered in Harry's ear.

"I should kill you now you miserable bastard… But that would be too good for you. You're going to jail for a long time you fucking prick and you're going to be the plaything of every fucking thug in Scotland. They will torture you till you break. And when you do – if they put you in a mental ward I'll be coming to get you. Your nightmare has just begun."

He grabbed a handful of Harry's hair and forced him to look into his face. "Do not forget this night Harry Ainsworth – you're a dead man walking."

Security staff were now pouring into the room and Lydia was already being carried quickly away. She hung pale and limp in a large security guards arms.

Loges saw the look of terror in Cameron's eyes.

"It's OK Cam – she's still with us – they're rushing her to the foyer – ambulances are already on their way."

Cameron struggled to make sense of this and was suddenly lost in the confusion around him. There were security men talking into his face but he couldn't hear them. The world was getting cloudy. His mates were holding him and talking directly to him but he could hear no words. He couldn't understand what was happening. The room spun and Cameron let go and slid into the darkness.

Chapter 23

Cameron had a splitting head-ache. He did not want to open his eyes. He was aware of people moving around him...and bright lights... He wished someone would switch off the frigging lights. His head felt like someone had driven an ice pick through it. His mouth was dry and he had itchy feet. Odd... Bloody sore head...

He felt someone squeeze his hand and opened his eyes just enough to investigate. Two blurred people were sitting beside his bed. There was humming machinery and a drip machine all around the bed with lights flashing and illuminated numbers flickering. He couldn't make sense of all this and slipped back into dozing where he could escape the pain in his head.

Sometime later he opened his eyes as a smiling young woman with skin as black as coal and eyes twinkling like diamonds wiped his forehead and tucked his bedclothes in around him. She smiled when she realised he was awake and said, "Hello Mr Veterinary...You look like you're feeling better now."

Cameron couldn't make sense of this at all. He stared at the smiling face and couldn't remember who she was. Was she from the Aboriginal Mission on the edge of town? Did she have a dog? A familiar voice boomed from the side of the bed.

"Hey Cambo. Good to see you at last. How are you feeling?"

Cameron moved his attention to the two people sitting close by the side of his bed. A big ugly bloke and a beautiful woman with the face of an angel. They both looked tired and their clothes were wrinkled and dishevelled. After a few seconds he recognised Logan Bloomsberry and his gorgeous wife Electra. Electra was holding his hand and squeezing it intermittently. They both looked gaunt and worried.

Cameron's brain finally kicked in. He croaked.

"Hi chaps... Must have been a good party..."

Logan and Electra both smiled. They suddenly looked relieved. He noticed tears welling in Logan's eyes. They all looked at one another for several minutes. Slowly memories of the previous evening crept back into Cameron's mind.

"They must have pumped me full of good shit... I feel rather fragile this morning..."

Logan looked serious.

"They overdosed you on heroin. You were not supposed to wake up..."

There were more long moments of silence.

"Lydia... Is she OK?" Cam whispered.

Logan seemed to steel himself before replying.

"She's alive Cam... Thanks to you... She's on life support. She's in both heart failure and renal failure. Nobody can tell how her brain function is yet. It might be days or weeks before we know. She was given the same heroin mix as you but probably an hour or so before. If she hadn't received the Naloxone in the ambulance on the way here she would not have made it. You saved her life Cam..."

Cameron stared at his friends and let the information sink in. He was remembering the details of the hours before he lost consciousness. He pictured the most beautiful woman he had ever laid eyes on smiling in his arms.

Tears started to cascade down his cheeks.

"Shona..?" he whispered, desperately hoping that his memories were merely some horrific nightmare.

Both Logan and Electra looked at him and sombrely shook their heads. No words. No-one could talk. No-one could understand the absurdity or the barbarity of her passing.

After a few moments Logan stated.

"Police tried to contact Randal this morning – in Switzerland. He's vanished. Disappeared in the middle of the night without a trace. Interpol are investigating... Looks like he might have known what was going down."

"Harry..?" Cameron asked.

"He's in hospital too. Two broken ribs and contusions to his testicles...Some Australian git manage to severely traumatise his wedding tackle...Well done son..." Logan paused and put his hand over Electra's hand which was still holding Cameron's tightly. He continued.

"Harry has been formally charged with Shona's murder. He has also been charged with attempted murder and grievous bodily harm to both you and Lydia. The video taken on your phone means he's going to jail for a very long time. The conference call we all listened too has resulted in murder investigations being opened into both Rachel and Damien's deaths. Harry is the prime suspect in both cases."

Electra squeezed Cameron's hand tightly. She added, "The bastard is going down Cameron. He's going down... And it's all thanks to you. You are a saint..."

Cameron whispered, "I'm no saint Electra. I can't believe this has all happened..."

Electra persisted, "No Cam...You have done the world a great favour. You are wonderful."

Cameron smiled for the first time, "Electra... Now maybe you'll realise you married the wrong bloke..."

All three smiled awkwardly.

Logan added his tuppence worth. "Now, now Electra - he's not that wonderful. If it wasn't for myself turning up with the cavalry it might all have been a very different story. I think that your choice in spouse is vindicated."

Electra hugged Logan and he kissed her gently on the forehead.

"What happened to the devil-woman Belinda?" Cameron asked.

Logan continued with a faint smile. "She's in hospital too. Seemingly she has a bizarre congenital abnormality..."

Both Cameron and Electra looked confused and stared at Logan expectantly.

He continued. "Seemingly you stabbed her in the penis... And it was quite erect at the time...She lost a couple of litres of blood. The stab wound also penetrated into her abdomen and perforated her large bowel. She... He... It...? Has undergone major surgery to repair the bowel and treat the associated peritonitis... She also has had microsurgery to repair her penis. Unfortunately it looks like she'll survive and it is very probable that her penis will return to normal function..."

He paused to let this information sink in, then went on.

"She will be formally charged with the attempted murders of both you and Lydia and as an accomplice in the murder of Shona. There are likely to be way more charges once Damien and Rachel's deaths are investigated further."

"What a grotesque human being..." muttered Cameron.

Logan continued.

"As of this morning NAVH's is under investigation for fraud, blackmail and extortion. Their assets have been frozen. The hospitals can continue to trade as normal but all contracts will be reassessed. Things are moving very fast. Two business partners in jail and the other one on the run. I feel NAVH's is about to crash and burn."

All three friends sat in silence and contemplated the ramifications of the last 24 hours. The world was about to change dramatically for many people. Shona's kids were now motherless. Their father was on the run from the police. Lydia...poor Lydia...only time would tell how she was going to fare. Her daughter needed her. Maybe the roles would be reversed. Both Harry and Belinda were going to jail for very long times...quite possibly the rest of their lives. Serves the bastards right... Many veterinarians across the country were going to hear the news today and find themselves free from blackmail... free of ridiculous constraints within the practices where they worked. People like Victor and Eleanor unknowingly would be released from future trauma. Italian Luigi would have to be careful to distance himself from his two new best friends. There would be many other invisible effects from the happenings of the last 24 hours that they would never know about. How many other people were under Harry and Belinda's evil spell? Hopefully, the world would now be a better place again.

Cameron had his own personal demons. He had thought he was falling in love again. He had found someone who had loved him from afar... Someone that he had adored for thirty years. Whether or not it could have evolved into anything he would never know. For a fleeting moment he had been the happiest man on the planet...He had loved the most perfect woman on the planet... Maybe she wasn't perfect. He knew that she probably wasn't... But the dream was delightful. He felt a cold space where he had excitedly nurtured a dream of happiness and love. She was gone forever. He was guilty of playing a part. He knew that Harry would have found a way to eliminate her from the picture whether he, Cameron, was here or not.

He felt guilt that he had welcomed the dream of love and happiness with another woman other than Alison... But his relationship with Alison was now changed forever. He knew that Alison probably had no knowledge that he had seen the video of her with her lover. Belinda had probably stolen the video from cyberspace and placed it in his e-mail as if it had been sent directly from Alison. The video, however it had arrived, had confirmed his suspicions. He felt sick. He felt abandoned. He felt used. But at least he knew now. It would be a difficult thing to go back to Australia – to Aiden Falls - and continue life in some form there and be happy. He knew his marriage was over... He had to go home and make it real.

Logan and Electra sat with Cameron in silence for probably another half hour before taking there leave. As they rose to leave Logan suddenly remembered a piece of news that he'd forgotten to tell Cameron.

"Sorry Cambo...Forgot to tell you... Pete was admitted to hospital last night too."

Cameron was suddenly worried.

"Oh shit... Is he OK? Not his heart?"

"No. no... I think you'd be quite proud of him. He broke 2 bones in his hand when he crash tackled Belinda and took her out during the battle last night... He's going to be fine. He's become a superhero too."

They all laughed and Logan and Electra took turns in hugging Cameron tightly before they left. Soon he was left staring at the walls and the surrounding machinery wondering how long he was expected to stay here.

There was a tap on the door and Cameron hoped that it would be a doctor to come and discharge him. He looked towards the door. The petite face of lovely Deirdre Micallef appeared.

She smiled when she saw him awake and asked, "Are you well enough for a visitor?"

"Of course Deirdre. Come on in."

She quietly entered the room. She was dressed conservatively in a black woollen skirt and a black blouse. She wore black flat shoes. She looked tired and had big bags under her eyes. Her eyes were bloodshot and he could make out light trails on her cheeks where tears had recently been spilled. If this was as bad as Deirdre could look she was a very lucky woman. Despite looking tired and distraught she was still stunning – she looked beautiful and broken all at the same time. She walked quickly to the bed and wrapped herself around Cameron. She cried and cried and her whole body shuddered and trembled as she did. He held her against him and kissed the top of her head.

Eventually she lifted her head and looked into his eyes.

"I'm so happy you're going to be OK Cameron. Just so happy. You did not deserve any of this." She cried more and dropped her head onto his chest again.

He held her gently. After a few minutes she lifted her head again.

"I think we all need to thank you. You saved Lydia's life and now Harry and NAVH's are going to be held accountable for all their hellish deeds. You deserve a medal…"

She continued, "I'll miss Shona. I truly loved her. She was dealt a ridiculously bad hand. Why, oh why can life be so cruel?"

Cameron gently kissed her on the forehead.

"Life can be an absolute bitch can't it?" he whispered.

She nodded slowly and stared into his eyes.

"I want you to remember something."

He looked at beautiful tear filled eyes and said, "Of course…"

She paused for a moment looking for the right words. "After all this mess is over and you've gone home and sorted out your problems with Alison you must let me know what you're doing. I'm going back to Shetland. I'm going to be honest and realistic. I'm not being the abused wife any more. I'm not going to take any more emotional blackmail. I'm going to look after myself… The kids are all self-sufficient now. I have tried my hardest for as long as I can. I have loved Allen for many years… Believe me I hate watching him suffering but I do not have to be made a scapegoat – I do not need to be blamed for everything… I do not have to live in a prison anymore."

She paused and looked at Cameron.

Cameron looked at her unblinking, unwavering.

"One day, if you are free again, I'd love to come and visit you in Australia…"

She left the words to hang in the air. There was no doubt about what she was suggesting. He looked at her. Her eyes were imploring him to agree. His brain was suffering from the roller coaster ride between euphoria and agony of the last twenty-four hours. At first his brain would just not appreciate the words. His brain did not want to accept the proposal as it feared he could be crushed again. He was still suffering badly from acute emotional trauma.

She smiled. He smelled her perfume. He enjoyed her hugging him very much. She was beautiful and fragile like himself. She was damaged goods trying to find a new future. Was she desperate? She had been planning to run away with Damien. If truth be told Deirdre would be one of his favourite women in the whole world. He knew she was a saint. He knew she was worn thin. He wasn't a saint by any stretch of the imagination - but he was worn extremely thin himself. A voice in his head announced." You'll never know unless you try…"

He quietly whispered to her. "I'd absolutely love that Deirdre."

She kissed him softy on the lips and then gently dropped her head on his chest.

Cameron dozed for the next half hour or so while Deirdre comforted herself in the warmth of his arms. Neither of the pair of them moved until the door of the room opened and the dark skinned, twinkly eyed nurse entered announcing, " I hope you're feeling better now Mr Veterinary. I might have to ask your friend here to leave for the minute or two. You have a couple of visitors that need to talk to you about a few things."

Two unshaved grey men in rumpled grey suits walked to the end of the bed and looked at Cameron with no emotion at all. They were both lean and haggard looking. The older of the two had yellow eyes and yellow teeth. The smell of stale cigarette smoke oozed from every pore. He looked about 80 but was probably in his early sixties. He had not worn well. The younger of the two – likely late thirties but aging rapidly like his partner - had coffee stains and toasts crumbs on his shirt below a crumpled tie.

The younger of the two spoke in a gruff Glasgow accent. "I'm Detective Baird and this is DCI Young of Scotland's Special Branch. If you could take your leave please miss we need to have a wee chat to Mr Woods here about his activities last night…"

He looked straight at Cameron and stated. "We understand that you haven't been back in the country for 24 hours yet sir… You seem to have been quite busy…"

Printed in Great Britain
by Amazon